D0428678

RUBY FINLEY VS. THE INTERSTELLAR INVASION

RUBY FINLEY VS. THE INTERSTELLAR INVASION

K. Tempest Bradford

Farrar Straus Giroux
New York

Farrar Straus Giroux Books for Young Readers
An imprint of Macmillan Publishing Group, LLC
120 Broadway, New York, NY 10271 • mackids.com

Library of Congress Cataloging-in-Publication Data
Names: Bradford, K. Tempest, 1978– author.
Title: Ruby Finley vs. the Interstellar Invasion / K. Tempest Bradford.
Other titles: Ruby Finley versus the Interstellar Invasion
Description: First edition. | New York : Farrar Straus Giroux Books for Young Readers, 2022. | Audience: Ages 8–12. | Summary: Eleven-year-old Ruby, a Black girl who loves studying insects, accidentally captures an alien bug, but when the creature escapes and starts wreaking havoc around the neighborhood, it is up to Ruby and her rag-tag group of friends to find this new invasive species before the feds do.
Identifiers: LCCN 2022006519 | ISBN 9780374388799 (hardcover)
Subjects: CYAC: Insects—Fiction. | Extraterrestrial beings—Fiction. | African Americans—Fiction. | Fiction. lcgft
Classification: LCC PZ7.1.B7269 Ru 2022 | DDC [Fic]—dc23
LC record available at https://lccn.loc.gov/2022006519

First edition, 2022
Book design by Aurora Parlagreco
Printed in the United States of America by Lakeside Book Company, Harrisonburg, Virginia

1 3 5 7 9 10 8 6 4 2

For my mother, who inspired me.
For my father, who gave me poetry.
And for the village, who raised me.

RUBY FINLEY VS. THE INTERSTELLAR INVASION

CHAPTER ONE

Ruby loved bugs. She loved the cool-looking ones and the creepy ones and the pretty ones and the huge ones. The ones with six legs and eight legs and a thousand legs and no legs. She loved looking at them and talking about them and learning about them and picking them up. That last one was usually what got her in trouble.

"Take that nasty thing outside!" Gramma would say (after she was done screaming in fright) when she found them in the Tupperware or the mason jars hidden under Ruby's bed or in the closet. Gramma had a No Tolerance policy when it came to bugs. Any sign of an ant in the bedroom, a housefly in the kitchen, spiders in the basement, or stink bugs on the windowsills, and she would hunt them down with no mercy, her homemade bug-killing juice in an old spray bottle in one hand and sometimes a mallet in the other.

So on that late-September afternoon when Ruby spotted the weirdest bug she'd ever seen in her front yard, she made sure no one sitting on their porch or walking down the street was looking. Then she scooped up the bug with a trowel and dropped it into one of the mason jars she kept hidden under the porch for just this sort of thing.

Slipping into the house by the side door so she wouldn't have to go past the TV room where Gramma was watching her stories, Ruby went upstairs (without thundering like an elephant) and dashed into her room. Here she had time to study the weird bug up close. It didn't look like any of the species she'd ever seen before. It was a dull red color and had six legs (so not a spider), big green eyes like a fly (but no wings), and a pinchy mouth like an ant (except no segments). She figured she should look it up to make sure it wasn't dangerous like those emerald ash borer beetles she found infesting the trees around the house. Her gramma was happy she'd been out there "messin' with them bugs" that day.

No matter what key words she put into her school tablet's search engine, the results didn't show anything even close to what was in front of her. Her daddy had given her a big book for identifying insects, arthropods, and other bugs, with pictures of almost every known tiny creature with four or more legs discovered around the world. After a half hour of flipping through it, she still hadn't found anything.

"What are you?" she asked it. The bug didn't answer.

Finally, she took a couple of pictures of it with the tablet and logged in to the secret Twitter account her parents didn't know she had. *Anyone seen an insect like this before?* she typed, then uploaded the pictures. She hit tweet, looked up from the tablet, and saw that the mason jar was empty.

"Uh . . ."

The top was still screwed on tight.

"But how . . . ?"

She picked up the jar and found a hole—a perfectly circular hole—in the side.

"What?"

A noise at the window made her look over. There was the weird bug, and it was using its front legs to burn a hole through the mesh screen.

"WHAT!"

It looked back at her, then leaped through the hole and outside. Ruby tore off down the stairs—"How many times have I told you not to run around this house like an elephant!"—and ran outside, but she saw no sign of the green-eyed, six-legged, glass-cutting, metal-burning bug.

Half an hour later, Ruby still hadn't found it and was sitting on the front porch trying to figure out how she was going to explain the hole in her window screen. Out of nowhere three black sedans came zooming down the street, pulled up in front of the house, and a bunch of white men in suits got out. This was never, ever a good thing, even in a safe neighborhood like hers.

"Grammaaaaaaaaa!" she shouted as she ran inside.

"What, girl, what is it?" Gramma asked, unconcerned until she saw the men on her porch. Her body went stiff and her expression turned stony. "Can I help you?"

One of the white men, with hair cut so short he was almost bald, stepped up to the door.

"Ma'am, I'm Agent Gerrold." He flashed a badge too fast to show what he was an agent of, exactly. "We're looking for . . ." He checked his smartphone, looked at Gramma over his dark glasses, then down to Ruby. "Are you @LilEntomologist on Twitter?"

"She's only eleven," Gramma said. "She ain't allowed on Twitter yet."

Agent Gerrold kept staring at Ruby.

"Yeah," Ruby admitted in a mumbly voice. She could already feel the whuppin' she was gonna get for creating another secret account.

"Where is this?" He turned his screen to show the picture of the bug she'd tweeted earlier.

"What in h—! What *is* that?" Gramma said in a very familiar-to-Ruby tone.

"I don't know where it is," she said. "It escaped after I posted that."

"Escaped where?" Gramma shrieked. "Is that thing somewhere in my house?!"

Ruby had a feeling she wasn't gonna be able to sit for a month. "No, Gramma! It ate through the screen and escaped out the window!" That was not the thing to say to make her calm down.

"Ate through?" Gramma looked like she was gonna drop to the floor right then.

"Ma'am." The agent stepped forward like he was fixing to catch her, then stepped back when she shot a look at him. "Ma'am, please stay calm. The specimen won't hurt you."

"The specimen?" Gramma and Ruby said at the same time.

"It's a Reduvius *Zelus longipes* bug from the Amazonian rain forest. They don't attack humans. They only use their powerful saliva to kill the other insects they eat and to escape from danger."

"So it's going to eat up my house?"

"No, ma'am. It only wanted to escape. It probably came in the house looking for warmth. They're not used to our climate. They're also skittish and don't like human contact, so it likely ran away from the structure."

The agent was talking in a calm and authoritative tone. Ruby recognized it from her mama, who used that voice on patients who were freaked out about going to the dentist. It was calming Gramma down, so Ruby didn't tell him that she knew he was talking nonsense. Reduvius *Zelus longipes* was the scientific name for a type of assassin bug. She'd read all about those. That thing she caught earlier didn't look anything like any assassin bug she'd ever seen a picture of.

Plus, who sent out three cars full of white men in suits to track down an assassin bug?

"The species is invasive and doesn't have natural predators here. To be safe, we're going to search the whole area and we need you to stay inside."

Gramma was calming down and starting to be skeptical again. "Over one bug from the Amazon?"

"They kill bees, ma'am," the agent said very seriously. "You know what will happen if the bees die."

That made Gramma gasp. Everyone in this house knew the importance of bees, thanks to Ruby.

"I understand," Gramma said, pulled her granddaughter inside, and closed the door.

CHAPTER TWO

Ruby and Gramma watched the G-men (as Gramma kept calling them) from the windows as they searched the neighborhood. Their house was near the corner, so from upstairs Ruby could track them pretty far down the block and on the cross street. They were using fancy equipment—far too fancy for finding a bug. Something else must be going on, but what?

She grabbed her tablet to see if anyone had responded to her tweet. No one had. In fact, the tweet was gone from her account. And before she had a chance to be mad about that, the tablet flashed a message that it was resetting to factory defaults.

"No, wait!" she yelled like it would do any good. It didn't. She didn't even have time to save the photos from the gallery. In a few seconds the tablet was rebooting, the little android's guts spinning and spinning on the screen.

The school had the ability to trigger a factory reset at any time, but they only bothered to do that when a tablet was stolen. Ruby peered out the window at the men, frowning. This was their fault. Somehow, they'd gotten into her Twitter account and her tablet and erased the evidence of the strange bug. No way this was some common assassin bug. Something big was going on.

The tablet would be useless for a while, so she turned on her xCUBE game console to see if any of her friends were on and chatting. Her cousin Hollie and friends Brandon and Alberto were in a voice chat room for the game *Neon Crisis Avengers*. When she entered, Ruby saw that only Alberto was playing—the other two were watching and talking.

". . . they're parked in front of Ruby's house. You think she's in trouble?" she heard Brandon say once she got in. He lived down the block and was always ready for someone else to be in trouble because then it wouldn't just be him.

"No, I'm not!" she said defiantly.

"But I bet you know what's going on," her cousin

Hollie said. "Where did all these white people come from?"

"I dunno. They said they're with the government. They came looking for that bug I tweeted about."

"You're back on Twitter?" Hollie now sounded all adult and fake disappointed.

"You're definitely gonna get in trouble," Brandon sang. Such a brat.

"Only if my parents find out."

"And they certainly will," Hollie said.

Brandon sucked his teeth. "Not you acting like you're not gonna be the one to tell them."

"I would never!" Hollie said. "Ruby's my bestie, I wouldn't get her in trouble on purpose. I'm just concerned." Hollie was only a year older than Ruby but she acted like she was grown. The way she said *concerned* sounded just like her mom, Ruby's aunt Peggy.

"As long as everyone keeps quiet there's no need for *concern*." Ruby mimicked Hollie, giggling. "Anyway, those government men are looking for the weird bug because they say it's dangerous to the environment."

"This feels extra for a single bug," Hollie said.

"Not if it's poisonous," Brandon said. "Or if it lays eggs inside of bird nests. Or if it crawls in your ear at night and eats your brain!"

"Brandon, ew! Why you always gotta be so revolting?" She could tell Hollie was scratching in her ear just thinking about it.

"Y'all are so distracting," Alberto said before yelling at an enemy who'd used a special move on him. "Die-die-die-die, you absolute . . . *asparagus!*"

"Please, you've played this level seventy million times and have it memorized," Hollie said. "Good save, though, did your papi walk in?"

"Yes," he said all terse. Alberto's fathers felt that his "foul language was getting out of control" and had been threatening to take his actual controllers away if he didn't clean up his language and stop cursing. He'd been getting creative about it ever since. "Leave me alone, I'm trying to beat the international high score!"

Alberto was the best gamer in school—in almost the whole city. He'd won three local tournaments and a few online ones. If his fathers weren't so overprotective he would have his own Twitch and YouTube channels and be an eSports star already, Ruby was sure of it.

"That bug they're looking for ain't poisonous and it won't eat your brain," Ruby said using her very grown-up scientist voice. Though she wasn't sure if what she was saying was true. Assassin bugs didn't eat brains but the thing she had caught was NOT an assassin bug.

She went over to the screen to study the hole it had made. A perfect circle. And the metal did look melty, like it had been burned. The mason jar's hole had smooth edges, too, not even a sliver of glass sticking out. Maybe that's what it looked like when glass melted. So this thing could generate heat with its legs? She decided not to mention that. Hollie was freaked out enough already.

When she put her headset back on, the game was paused and their friends Jackie and Mayson had come into the chat.

"They told us we had to stay inside for safety and my mom is mad," Mayson was saying. She lived on the next street over and the G-men had just started closing off traffic there and sweeping backyards with the instruments. "She says it's a government plot to get into our business."

"Your mom thinks everything's a government plot," Brandon said.

"Your mama—" Mayson started, but she was drowned out by a horn noise that made Ruby wince and pull her headset partially off.

"You know the rules!" Jackie, the originator of the noise, said. "No Yo Mama jokes in this chat. We don't want another incident."

That was true. None of them wanted to relive the great Yo Mama war of Christmas break. It had lasted over a month, with the insults going from funny to convoluted and finally to downright mean. Feelings got hurt and people stayed mad for days. It got so bad that their actual mamas had to get involved and broker a peace. That's when they made the rule: no Yo Mama jokes and no "fake" trash talk in game chat. Not among themselves, at least.

"Fine," Mayson said. "My mom is right, anyway."

If eye-rolls had a noise they all made it. Mayson's mom was one of the only white people who lived in the neighborhood and everyone thought she was odd. She watched the *Strange Truth: Fact or Fiction* TV show and read lots of books about UFOs, so of course she went right to conspiracies.

"Those men are in my backyard right now," Alberto said, resuming the game. "If they mess up my papi's garden they better pray he never finds them."

Ruby heard Gramma coming up the stairs talking on the phone. "They're all the way over there? Lord Jesus, all this fuss over a bug."

"Whatever's going on I hope they get done soon. My dad was about to go to the store," Brandon said.

"Out of Brie again?" Hollie teased.

"As a matter of fact, yes. We need it to make our pear-and-Brie tart for dessert."

"You and your weird fancy food."

"Hey, you leave his fancy food alone," Ruby said. Brandon may have been a brat, but he loved to cook, just like his parents. She appreciated the scientific approach he took to it. Plus, he always shared the left-overs at lunch.

"Who you talking to?" Gramma asked, poking her head into the room.

"Hollie and them."

Gramma nodded and was about to leave when she spotted the hole in the screen. "What in—Is that what that thing did??"

"Gotta go." Ruby logged off, not wanting to give Brandon any more ammo.

"How big was that thing!" Gramma said, pointing to the two-inch-wide hole. It was just big enough to horrify.

"I don't know, I didn't get a good look." She slid the mason jar under the bed with her foot while Gramma was focused on the screen.

"They better find that thing." Now she was looking down at the men who were still searching the back-yard next door. A couple of them went across the street toward Witchypoo's.

No one had properly seen Witchypoo since before Ruby was born. The only time she appeared at her door was to call for her dogs or to bring her mail and groceries in, and she only did those things when it was near dark. Her yard was crowded with big trees, bushes, and overgrown grass; the house covered in vines and weeds. Even when she did step out you still might not see her. Witchypoo never let anyone in and everyone in the neighborhood avoided her house—Ruby and her friends never even went past it on the same side of the street.

The older kids had told them Witchypoo would hide in the bushes and jump out to grab you if you walked by. Plus, she had two big, mean dogs that she left loose in the unfenced backyard. They loved to chase kids riding by on bikes.

Gramma sucked her teeth. "Good luck searching in *that* jungle."

The G-men didn't get the chance. As soon as they got near the house, the dogs came around from the other side barking and growling. The men stopped and looked like they were discussing what to do about them when an old Black woman came out the back door to add to the noise.

That has to be Witchypoo, Ruby thought. She

definitely looked like a witch, wearing only a housecoat and a worn scarf that barely contained her ratty gray hair.

"Get on outta here!" she yelled at them. It was almost funny—a tiny Black woman waving her arms around trying to chase away two big government men. Except those men were white, and who knows what they would do to her . . . or the dogs.

"Oh Lord, I'd better go out there," Gramma said.

"But they said to stay inside."

"We all gonna have more problems than invasive species if she keeps going on like that. *You* stay here." She started dialing someone on the phone as she went. "And put some tape over that hole. Don't need any other bugs getting in."

Ruby taped up the screen while watching what went down. Gramma marched outside and got between Witchypoo and the men. She was trying to order both of them around at once, telling Witchypoo to take the dogs inside while also telling the men they needed to back off until she did. The men were also yelling, telling Gramma to step back and warning Witchypoo that she needed to get her animals under control. The dogs were mad at everybody and getting madder by the second. After a couple minutes the agent who had come to

Ruby's door showed up and waved the other men off. Once they moved to the other side of the street Agent Gerrold stepped back and let Gramma convince Witchy-poo to come inside. She finally went . . . after making a bunch of rude gestures that would have gotten Ruby punished for life.

And, after all that, the G-men were careful to stay on the sidewalk when they scanned the edges of the old woman's property.

Even the government was scared of Witchypoo.

CHAPTER THREE

Since the G-men weren't letting anyone down their street, Ruby's parents both arrived home late and at the same time, which didn't happen often. They were complaining about the delay as they walked in the door and both of them were big mad.

"He kept my ID for over half an hour, like the address was gonna magically change to something else the longer he held on to it," Mama said to Gramma.

"They were running background checks, I bet." Daddy's voice was calm, but with a tone Ruby recognized as held-back anger. It was the way he talked when people on the City Council were trying to pull "some shady stuff" on him or other community organizers.

"Mama, are you sure this is just about finding an insect?" she said to Gramma.

"That's what they told us when they first got here. They had a picture of it, asked where it was."

"They asked you? Why? Where'd they get a picture?" Daddy asked.

"Ruby put it on Twitter."

As soon as her gramma said that all eyes turned to Ruby and all hope of not getting in trouble over this vanished.

Gramma did look apologetic. She probably hadn't planned to mention Ruby's Twitter account since so much else was going on.

"Ruby. Again?" was all Mama said.

Now the anger was on Daddy's face as well as in his voice. "What did we say the last time you made a Twitter account?"

"You are too young to be on Twitter and, when you are old enough, you can only have an account that we monitor," Ruby recited in a monotone mumble.

"And why is that?"

"Because social media is unsafe for young kids and it's our job to help you stay safe."

"How is it that you can remember what we say word

for word and still do exactly what we told you not to do?" Mama asked.

The real answer was: *Because I didn't think you'd find out this time.* But Ruby was sure that wouldn't be a good thing to say. "I want to talk to other people in the Bug Club and no one is on the forums anymore!"

All the adults groaned in exasperation. This was an old fight. Ever since they let Ruby join the Midwestern Amateur Entomologist Society she'd been begging her parents to let her on social media. The forums got a few posts a month, but all the really interesting stuff was on Twitter and Instagram. Despite this fact, Mama and Daddy were adamant that she would have to wait. How else was Ruby supposed to react to this unfairness but to create secret accounts?

"Baby girl, I don't like this habit you've developed of lying and going behind our backs," Mama said. "How are we supposed to trust you when you keep doing things like this?"

"I'm sorry," she said in her best I'm-an-innocent-little-girl-aren't-I-cute? voice.

"Your apology is accepted, but it won't—" Daddy stopped at the sound of several loud voices in the yard behind theirs. They all rushed to the window to see what was going on.

One of the G-men was holding a metal box that looked built to contain nuclear waste, not a small insect. "Got it!" he kept calling out to the others, who converged on him with their scanning instruments.

"Thank goodness that's over. Now they can leave," Gramma said.

Mama leaned closer to the glass. "Why did they bring such a big box? How big is this bug?"

"Not *that* big," Ruby said.

"Yeah, I don't trust this at all," Daddy said, and she agreed.

A few minutes later someone knocked on the door. It was Agent Gerrold again.

"Mr. and Mrs. Finley. Mrs. Larkin. Wanted you to know we found the insect before it could do any more damage," he said.

None of the adults looked impressed or relieved. That didn't seem to upset him.

"It's a good thing Ruby here found it when she did. This could have been a much worse situation without her help."

Then why did you delete my pictures and tweet? Ruby wanted to ask. She didn't think he would answer her honestly, so she only said: "Thanks."

"Does this mean we're allowed to leave the house now?" Daddy asked.

"Yes sir," Agent Gerrold said, and Daddy raised his eyebrows, surprised. "You folks take care. Sorry for the inconvenience."

They watched all the men get into their black cars and drive away before going back in.

"That . . . was strange," Mama announced.

"At least it's done," Gramma said, heading into the kitchen. She'd been keeping dinner warm for them.

Daddy didn't look convinced. He had his I'm-gonna-take-this-up-with-my-councilwoman expression on. That is, until Mama kissed his beard and smoothed it away. "Think about it tomorrow."

Ruby wrapped her arms around his belly and squeezed. "Yeah, don't worry, Daddy."

He leaned over and kissed the top of her head, his long dreds falling down to tickle her face. "You know I love you, right?"

"Yep!"

"More than anything in the whole world."

"Even more than ribs," she said.

"That's right." He kissed her again. "But you're still grounded."

CHAPTER FOUR

After much discussion, Ruby's parents and Gramma decided on her punishment. No spanking this time (Mama didn't approve of it, though she made it clear a third strike would put spanking back on the table). Instead, Ruby was sentenced to a month of no unsupervised computer or tablet time, a week without TV, and two weeks without her xCUBE.

"But how am I supposed to chat with my friends?" she whined when that announcement came down.

"There's this amazing invention called the telephone," Mama said. "You can use it to speak to people up the street or all the way across town."

Ruby held back from rolling her eyes. Only old people used the phone to talk to each other.

The next morning she walked down the block to her cousin Hollie's house. It was Saturday, so Ruby knew she'd be playing xCUBE with the others. Hollie's mom, Aunt Peggy, answered the door and gave her a big hug.

"Just so you know, your mama told me about your punishment," she said. Ruby groaned. Did everyone have to know? "No tryna sneak on the game box while you're here."

"Yes ma'am," she said, resigned.

"They found out, huh," Hollie said when Ruby walked into the TV room.

"Gramma told on me."

"They always find out eventually."

"They wouldn't have if those stupid G-men hadn't shown up."

"G-men?"

Ruby shrugged. "That's what Gramma called them."

"Yeah, she's here. Hold on," Hollie said into her headset, then she paused the game. "How long will you be on punishment?"

"No xCUBE for two weeks, no unsupervised tablet for a *month*."

Brandon laughed so loud she could hear it from the headphones.

"Shut UP!" she leaned into the mic to shout. Hollie

pushed her away playfully. "Ask them if they'll come out. We could go to the playground or something."

"Fiiiine," Hollie said. "Jackie says yes, too. Brandon says no and, guess what, no one cares. Alberto says he'll meet us there. He's going to the store first. And now Brandon is coming anyway."

"Okay. We should go by Mayson's and see if she wants to come."

"I suppose." Hollie rolled her eyes. She didn't like Mayson as much as Ruby did but, because she was a good cousin and best friend, she didn't complain about it. Too often.

Ruby felt bad for Mayson. Unlike her, Hollie, Jackie, Alberto, and Brandon, she hadn't grown up in the neighborhood. She and her folks moved in two years back, and that combined with her being the youngest and half white and going to a different school than most of them made her an outsider. Ruby knew what that felt like. Over the summer between fourth and fifth grades, two of her best school friends had decided they didn't like her anymore for some reason and shut her out. If she hadn't had her friends on the block, she would have been alone and sad the whole summer. She made sure to include Mayson whenever they were all doing something together so she wouldn't feel that way.

They met up at the playground at the old elementary school in the middle of the neighborhood. It had been decommissioned after Ruby's third-grade year and replaced by a new building up Reading Road. The old building hadn't been torn down yet and the playground was still intact, so their parents let them play there.

Brandon and Jackie were already on the swings when they rolled up.

"I'm gonna beat your record!" Brandon said to Jackie, kicking the swing high and jumping off, landing just shy of the grass at the edge of the gravel.

"Not even close!" Jackie was the oldest of them and the tallest and had jumped the farthest off the swing—all the way into the grass. No way were any of them going to match her anytime soon. A point she proved by landing almost two feet past Brandon when she jumped.

"Woo! Go Jackie!" Mayson cheered.

Brandon rolled his eyes and started saying something about how he could still jump farther than any of the rest of them.

"You got your hair cut," Jackie said over him, talking to Mayson. "It looks cute!"

"Thanks," she said, fluffing up the loose curls into a halo around her head. "I finally convinced my mom this would be the easiest to maintain."

Ruby went to get on the swing Brandon had abandoned and watched Mayson preen. Since Jackie was the oldest as well as the tallest, she was kind of the leader of their crew. No one minded since she looked out for them, kept the older kids from messing with them, and kept the peace between them. Ruby thought Mayson idolized her a little and maybe that was the reason she wanted her hair short. Jackie's was, too, and she kept it in cornrows most of the time so it seemed even shorter.

Hollie passed the swings up to inspect the new chain and padlock someone had put on the school doors. No one was supposed to go inside, so of course a bunch of people tried. Usually older kids, and usually to do stuff they weren't supposed to do. Hollie's older brother, Frankie Lee, had been caught there twice, the second time because she told on him.

"You checking to make sure it's secure, Officer?" Brandon yelled out. "Always lookin' to tattle on somebody."

Hollie flipped her long braids and made a point of ignoring him.

"Who did she tell on this time?" Alberto said, riding up with a bag full of candy. "Is she why Ruby is on punishment?"

"No!" Hollie and Ruby said together.

"The reason I'm in trouble is those government men." Ruby was still resentful. "They told Gramma about my Twitter account."

"Which you were forbidden to have." It was like Hollie couldn't help herself.

Alberto rolled his eyes and handed Ruby a chocolate bar. "To tide you over in these hard times." Then he whispered, "Sometimes she can be an absolute toenail."

Ruby giggled. "At least *someone* feels sorry for me."

Out of all the boys in her grade, Ruby liked Alberto the best. He was nice to everyone and didn't act any different around girls than he did around other guys. She also appreciated that, like her, he was shorter than most of the other sixth graders. She still had half an inch on him, though.

"My papi is so mad at those government goons," he said. "They messed up the fence around our garden searching for that bug and last night the cats got in."

"They didn't eat the collards, did they?" Brandon asked, seriously upset.

"They peed on them, man."

Brandon growled in frustration. "Your papi was gonna let me use them for that spring roll recipe!"

"Lo siento," Alberto said sympathetically.

"They didn't get all the way down to our house. I

bet my mother would have lost it if they'd come into our yard and messed stuff up like that," Jackie said.

"She could have sicced Ruby's bees on them," Mayson said. "My mom said they deserved it when they got stung."

"They didn't mess with the hive in your backyard, did they?" Ruby hadn't thought of that until now. She needed those bees for her science fair project. Mayson's and Jackie's parents had both allowed the Cincinnati Urban Beekeepers Alliance to set up hives in their yards and let Ruby help care for them so she could run her big experiment. She wanted the first hive in her yard, but Gramma was scared of getting stung. The other one had to be far enough down the block so the hives wouldn't compete for the same food sources.

"No, they were careful, my mom had eyes on them the whole time."

"I heard Witchypoo sicced her dogs on 'em," Jackie said.

"She tried to," Ruby said. "Gramma got her to take them inside."

"The one time those stupid mutts could be useful . . ." Brandon muttered.

"Two dogs versus men with guns? I don't think so," Hollie said.

"Wait, I thought you said they were looking for a bug," Jackie said. "Why did they have guns?"

"The FBI always carries guns."

Alberto shook his head. "They weren't the FBI, they were from Homeland Security. They told my dad when they came in the yard."

"They told my brothers they were from the Department of Fish and Wildlife," Brandon said.

"What'd they tell you?" Jackie asked Ruby.

"They didn't. The man who came to our door just said he was an agent."

"They were probably from the CIA," Mayson said in a way that sounded like she was repeating something her mom told her. Miz Trish was always going on about stuff like that.

"FBI, CIA, NCIS, whoever they were, it's still Ruby's fault they showed up," Brandon said.

"It is not!" Ruby play-punched him in the arm. "Besides, it's a good thing they came, isn't it? What if that bug had been dangerous?"

"Then it would be a terrible idea to bring it in the house . . ." Hollie pointed out.

Ruby stuck out her tongue.

"Wait, you took that bug into your house?" Alberto asked. "Why?"

Hollie pulled a face. "Hello, have you met her?"

"Why not keep it in the garage or something?"

"I can't take my books or my tablet out to the garage, it's gross in there," Ruby said.

"But it's not gross to store bugs in jars under your bed." Jackie was teasing, she knew. Still, why didn't anyone get it? The best way to learn was to observe and experiment. Sometimes that meant bringing specimens into the lab. She didn't have a lab yet, so her bedroom would have to do.

"How long are you on punishment?" Mayson asked.

"No xCUBE for two weeks. Will y'all do stuff with me IRL until it's over?"

They all said yes, though Ruby wasn't sure if they would. Even though they lived within two blocks of each other they'd spent most of their time together online and in games since the xCUBE came out three Christmases ago. What if they forgot about their promise and she had to spend the next two weeks alone?

🕷 🕷 🕷

What happened after church the next day didn't make Ruby feel any better. She tried to convince the others to come over to her house, but they all wanted to watch Alberto stream his speedrun through the most difficult level in *Tyger Bright 3*. Hollie promised to come over after, but that didn't take the sting out of it. And even though it wasn't *technically* on TV and Ruby wasn't *technically* playing herself, her parents said that she couldn't watch and no amount of begging made them change their minds. With nothing fun to do and no one to do it with, Ruby ended up sitting on the porch listening to her gramma gossip with the other church ladies.

Miz Connor, Miz Ella, Jackie's mom, Miz Pam, and Gramma all went to different churches, so they got together after service to trade stories about who in the congregation was doing what and why. Mayson's mom, Miz Trish, also joined them, though she didn't go to church. Ruby's mama said she just liked talking.

That day the five of them weren't gossiping about their friends but about the G-men. And when Miz Ella went to show them a post she had made about it on Facebook, it was gone.

"Gone?" Gramma said, taking her phone out. "I just saw it yesterday!"

"It says the post violated community guidelines and they removed it," Miz Ella read off the screen.

"That don't make no kind of sense!" Miz Connor grabbed the phone from Ella, who gave her an annoyed look. "What guideline did the post violate?"

"It won't say. It never says. I'm so tired of Facebook," Miz Pam said, checking her own.

"They took mine down, too!" Gramma said.

Just like my Twitter post, Ruby thought, though she didn't say so out loud. No point in getting a talking-to from everyone. Still, this was weird. All the Facebook posts the ladies had made about the neighborhood lockdown were gone.

"This is government overreach!" Miz Trish said when she saw hers had been deleted, too.

Miz Pam sucked her teeth at that. All the adults side-eyed Trish's conspiracy talk. "Why do they care if we post about them? Not like it was a secret, they had the street closed off forever."

"Maybe because they don't want people to know what they were really looking for," Miz Trish said. Gramma threw her hand dismissively, but Miz Trish wasn't dissuaded. "You said it ate through a window screen!"

They all looked up at that, now not so quick to dismiss her. Ruby wondered if she should mention that the men had lied about the kind of bug it was.

"This has government cover-up written all over it," Miz Trish went on. "They weren't looking for some insect. I think it was something that escaped. From a lab, maybe."

"They did call it a 'specimen,'" Ruby said. All the women looked over at her and she shrugged. "They did!"

"See!" Trish's green eyes lit up like they always did when she really got going. "A specimen. That escaped."

"Let's hope they keep it locked up." Miz Connor now sounded convinced. The other ladies didn't seem as sure.

"Did y'all see this?" Miz Pam turned her screen around to show them a picture from the car repair place next to the corner store. Their fence had a hole in it.

"What happened now?" Gramma asked.

Miz Pam scrolled down. "Says someone broke in last night and stole hubcaps, spare parts . . . but none of the money."

"Speaking of things that don't make sense," Miz Ella said, shaking her head.

"Why would someone take that stuff and not money?" Ruby asked.

"Maybe they couldn't get to it," Gramma said.

"Or maybe there's something unnatural going on over there," Miz Trish said, sounding like one of those *UFO Secrets Exposed!* people.

All the other women exchanged looks but didn't answer her. Still, between the government men lying and everyone's social media posts disappearing, Ruby wondered if Miz Trish might be right.

CHAPTER FIVE

The next day at school Ruby couldn't wait for science class. She wanted to talk to her teacher about the weird bug and see if she would help figure out what it was. Mrs. Bailey was a tall white woman with the thinnest lips Ruby had ever seen. She was always pinching them up when the kids in class didn't act right. And since Brandon was also in this class, that happened almost every day. She wasn't as friendly or encouraging as Ruby's elementary school science teacher had been, but she was still a scientist, so Ruby knew she would want to help.

During class she didn't get a chance to ask about it because Mrs. Bailey got them started on an experiment with circuits right away. Once the bell rang, Ruby asked if she could stay behind to talk.

"Is this about your science fair project proposal? Because it needs some work."

"No, it's—" Ruby frowned. "Wait, why does it need work?"

"This is a completely unrealistic project for you," Mrs. Bailey said, pulling out the sheet Ruby had turned in the week before. "Training bees to identify chemicals? That would take months of work and you'd need access to beehives and special clothes and equipment—"

"I know. I already do. I started the first stage of the experiment this summer." Information she'd put in the proposal. Ruby didn't understand why her teacher hadn't seen it.

"In your backyard," she said, disbelieving.

"Not mine, my neighbors'."

"Right. This is still too ambitious a project."

"It needs to be to qualify for District Science Day. I want to get a high enough score so I can go to State Science Day." Aside from winning scholarship money, students who placed high at the state level got the chance to attend advanced-level science camps.

"Is that a realistic goal for you?"

Why wouldn't it be? Ruby thought. "Yeah . . ."

Mrs. Bailey pinched her lips. "I think you should pick a different project. One from the list I provided you last week." She pulled out the sheet and handed it to Ruby. "One that will reflect well on the school."

Ruby wasn't sure what that meant. But she was sure she wasn't about to do one of the projects listed here. "None of these are interesting and none of them are about insects."

"Just take another look and consider it, okay?"

"I'll consider it." Saying that always made adults happy. Considering wasn't a yes or no. Considering wasn't a promise.

Still, all through lunch she stewed over what Mrs. Bailey had said. It didn't make sense for her to not want Ruby to do a hard project. Wasn't that the point of science fairs? Did she not think Ruby was smart enough? She got As on all her tests in science. What else did she need to do? Halfway through the period Ruby realized that she hadn't even had a chance to ask about the bug. Even worse.

* * *

There was one other person she could ask for help: Mr. Lewis, her science teacher from elementary school. When she graduated, he told her that she had been "a delight to teach" and even helped her come up with the idea to use bees in her middle school experiment.

Since he lived nearby he had given her permission to call or come visit if she needed help. But his house was on the other side of Paddock Road, and Ruby wasn't allowed to cross any major streets by herself or without permission.

After school she used her most polite voice to ask Gramma if she could visit Mr. Lewis.

"Get your homework and your chores done first. And you can only go if Hollie goes with you."

Tearing her cousin away from the xCUBE was harder. Ruby had to promise to buy her a pop from the store on their way back and farm some gold for her in *Papyri of Ptah* once she was off punishment. Promise made, they rode their bikes over to the other side of the neighborhood.

They found Mr. Lewis working in his garden. When he saw them he waved and smiled, making Ruby feel better immediately. He reminded her of her grandpa who had died—same wide smile and same wide nose.

"Hey girls, what's up?"

"You remember when those men from the government showed up Friday?" Ruby said.

"Yes," he said, now frowning. "They blocked off your street, right?"

"It's her fault," Hollie said.

"It's not, they came because of the bug!"

"What?" he asked, confused.

Ruby told Mr. Lewis the story, including the part about how the bug escaped.

"It burned a hole in the window screen?" he asked, eyes widening.

"You didn't tell me that part!" Hollie said.

"Or it chewed through it or something." Ruby shrugged, ignoring Hollie.

"That doesn't sound like any insect I've ever heard of. Describe it to me."

"Red, with six legs articulated in the middle. And it had mandibles like an ant. Green, mirrory eyes."

Hollie shivered like it was right in front of her. "Disgusting!"

"Hush!" Ruby said.

Mr. Lewis chuckled. "Did you get a picture?"

"Yeah, but my tablet reset to factory and I lost it."

"Too bad." He was quiet for a minute. "I'll try doing a search in the library database, see what I can find. I suggest you draw what you saw as best you can and upload the picture to the Bug Club forum."

Ruby groaned. She wasn't that good at drawing yet, though she practiced a bunch because Mr. Lewis told her it was a useful skill for entomologists. She also groaned because no one would see the picture in the forums.

"I'll tell the folks on Twitter to go look and help you," he said, smiling. "And for the record: I agree with your parents. You're too young to be on social media."

Ruby rolled her eyes at Hollie's smug "I told you."

"Can I ask one more favor?"

"Sure, but then you'd better get home," he said, pointing to the streetlight that had just come on.

"My teacher doesn't like my idea for the science fair, but I don't want to change it. Will you help me put it together if she won't?"

"Of course. But why doesn't she like it?"

Ruby shrugged again. "She says it's too ambitious for me."

"That's odd . . ." A concerned look crossed his face for a second. "Well, don't worry, I'll help you."

"Thanks," she said, and gave him a big hug. With him on her side there was no way Mrs. Bailey could stop her.

CHAPTER SIX

Being on punishment sucked. It had only been three days since Daddy unhooked the xCUBE and put a parental lock on her tablet, and Ruby was already suffering from the lack of games in her afternoon. It was almost a physical itch; one she couldn't scratch. And worse: hardly anyone felt sorry for her.

Monday she went over to Jackie's house like she did every weekday to check on the beehive she was using for her science project. Before they put on the protective clothing and went out, Jackie's other mama, Miz Shirley, made them a snack. She turned off the kitchen TV and looked pointedly at Ruby when she set the chips and queso in front of them.

"You need to stay off Twitter, Queen Bee," she warned.

"She won't let me get on Instagram, either," Jackie whispered when her mama's back was turned. "Even though I'm old enough."

"I'll decide when you're old enough."

Later, they went out to the backyard to check on the hive. The bees were calm, going about their bee business. That past summer Ruby had trained the forager bees to come to a specific feeder, which they checked on next. Two weeks before she'd started adding ammonia to the area around the sugar water so the bees would associate the scent with a reward. The hardest part was marking the bees with a bit of color so she knew which ones to capture later. Miz Shirley helped her when the bulky protective covering she had to wear made it difficult.

After, Ruby stuck around for a while to listen to Jackie practice speaking German. She went to a language-immersion school and already knew French and Spanish—that one made Alberto happy, since it meant he and Jackie could say secret things in front of everyone else (which drove Brandon nuts). He and his papi were Mexican, and so he taught Jackie about the differences of the language in his dialect.

Of all the languages Jackie knew, Ruby thought German was the funnest. She might learn it someday, though she would probably try Latin first. It was the language of science, after all.

She went to Hollie's next, hoping to drag her off the xCUBE by force. It wasn't about to happen.

"I'm gonna beat Brandon at this if it kills me." The two of them were going at it in *Basketball Apocalypse*.

"When you're done this level, will you come over?" Ruby pleaded.

"You're the one on punishment, not me," Hollie said.

"Rude!"

"I'll come over tomorrow, I promise." Hollie was quiet for a second—Brandon must have been saying something in the headset. "I am *not* gonna repeat that to her."

"Beat him double for me," Ruby said.

Hollie laughed. "Okay. And tomorrow, I pinkie promise."

Back at home, Ruby tried to distract herself by making a drawing of the bug like Mr. Lewis suggested. It only added to her frustration. Every time she tried, Ruby messed some part up, or it didn't look exactly the way she saw it in her head.

After two days of drawing she finally made something that looked right enough, and she uploaded it to the Bug Club forums. When she called Mr. Lewis so he could tweet about it, he had other news for her.

"I looked up the rules and if your science teacher won't approve your project, we can submit it to the district Science Council for approval. I'll email the form to your father."

"Do you think they'll approve it?" Ruby asked.

"Oh yes. I'll add my own letter of recommendation if need be," he said.

At least there was a tiny bit of good news.

That Wednesday evening Hollie and Alberto came over with their parents, who'd been invited along with half the neighborhood to an emergency community meeting her daddy had organized. They tried to play a board game in the basement while the adults talked, but they kept being interrupted by Gramma calling for Ruby or Hollie to get people pop or refill the snack trays. Alberto was exempt from this only because he was technically a guest.

"What are they talking about?" he asked when the girls finally came back down.

"A bunch of thefts," Ruby said. "They started this past weekend."

Hollie listed them off. "The car repair place Saturday night, then Sunday someone stole copper fittings from the new daycare going up on Reading Road. Monday someone broke into the plumbing supply up on Paddock and stole pipes. And last night part of the iron fence around the Episcopal church disappeared."

"Disappeared?" Alberto didn't look like he believed that one.

"Yup. Deacon Burke said it looked like someone sawed through it but no one heard anything like that, so they can't figure out how the thief did it," Ruby said.

Hollie rolled the dice, hoping to get back to their game. "Or why. There's nothing over there but a baby playground and the gazebo for wedding pictures. Three, four, five, YES! I get the first tower."

"Ugh, you absolute *toothbrush*." Alberto groaned.

They were just settling back into the game when Ruby heard Mama call her name. Again.

"Oh my gaaaawd," she said softly before yelling, "Yes ma'am?"

"I'm sorry, baby," Mama said from the top of the stairs. "Can you come up here and show Daddy how to broadcast his tablet to the TV? He forgot."

"Coming," she said, and pretended not to be annoyed with all the up and down. While she was making the tablet connection work, her daddy passed out some papers.

"This is a cheat sheet for filling out police reports in a way they can't easily dismiss."

"Not sure it'll do any good," Deacon Burke muttered.

"I know it doesn't seem like it," Daddy said, "but if we make sure to detail everything, there's a paper trail. That'll help Harshaw and the Community Care Program put pressure on Councilwoman Fudge if the cops don't do their job and follow up."

"They have to pay attention to this. A break-in every night this week? That's not normal. That wasn't even normal when we were kids." Sam, Alberto's Black dad, had grown up in Bond Hill, just like Ruby's mama. He and Daddy formed the neighborhood association way back before Ruby was born and had worked hard to make Bond Hill safe and to support businesses owned by Black people. Most of the break-ins were at those same businesses.

"Here, Daddy." Ruby held the tablet out. "I got it connected."

"Thanks, love." He gave her a kiss on the cheek before opening up a plan of action for the neighborhood watch.

Back down in the basement Ruby tried to get her head in the game again. She kept being distracted by a thought—one the adults didn't seem to be considering:

all these break-ins started after the government men came looking for the bug. Could they be behind it all, like Miz Trish thought?

But Mr. Lewis had taught Ruby that correlation didn't equal causation. Just because things happened around the same time didn't mean that one had anything to do with the other. Maybe it was a coincidence.

CHAPTER SEVEN

Thursday after school no one would come hang out with her and Ruby was totally, utterly despondent, lying on the floor of the living room groaning that she had no friends and would die alone, while her Gramma muttered, "Lord Jesus, this child."

"I'm so bored!" Ruby complained.

Gramma shook her head, unsympathetic. "Is your homework done?"

"Yes."

"And your chores?"

"Yes."

"I can always give you a few more . . ."

"I'm gonna go ride my bike," Ruby said, hopping up quickly.

She heard Gramma suck her teeth and say, "That's what I thought," as she escaped out the side door.

But with no one to ride or play with, Ruby wasn't sure where to go. She cycled around the old school a few times, still thinking about the break-ins and whether they were related to the other weird stuff that had happened lately, like the bug and the G-men.

Whenever scientists needed answers to mysteries, they relied on the scientific method. No reason she couldn't apply that here, Ruby figured. She'd already done the first step: Ask questions. Next was research and to make observations. Then you made a hypothesis based on that, tested your hypothesis, and made a conclusion.

She rode over to the car repair place and found the owner, Mr. David, working on a truck. He'd been one of her grandpa's best friends and always treated her like family. "Hey Ruby," he said when she skidded to a stop.

"Would it be okay for me to go look at the place where those burglars messed up your fence to get at the car parts they took?" she asked after giving him a hello hug.

"Why?"

"I'm doing a science project." That wasn't *quite* a lie. Plus, adults were always more helpful if they thought you were doing a school thing. "We have to research a topic and then make a hypothesis. I decided to research the places that have been broken in to."

"Okay, Scooby-Doo, I'll show you. Just be careful how you go about this," he warned, walking her toward one side of the lot. "Don't go anywhere folk can't see you. Just in case."

"Yes sir, I promise."

Now it was time for her to make observations. The hole in the chain-link fence had been patched with barbed wire, which Ruby also promised not to touch. Even with the repair, she could still see what had happened. Someone had cut a hole in the wire—one that didn't look very big. It was hard to estimate how big it had been before since whoever or whatever it was had pushed the hole bigger than the width of a basketball going out. She could tell since the edges of the cut metal were bent toward the street, not toward the lot.

Looking around the area Ruby didn't see anything else strange. There weren't many cars or spare parts back here anymore, probably because Mr. David had had the other mechanics move as much as they could into the building.

Ruby thanked him as she rode off to check out another place that had been broken into: the new daycare building. She didn't know any of the people working on the construction, so for a few minutes she hovered on the other side of a CAUTION tape and tried to spot where the break-in had happened. Not long after, she heard raised voices inside the almost-finished building. Two white men came out—a tall, burly one and a shorter man whose fancy suit clashed with his hard hat—and strode over to a large shipping container.

"You said this thing was high security!" the burly man said. "And you guaranteed it up to ten thousand."

"The *lock* is guaranteed, Mr. Fisher. The lock is intact." The suited man waved a metal circle at the other guy. It was bigger than an extra-large pizza and looked like it came from the side of the container.

"You know that's some weaselly crap, Smithson! There has to be something wrong with this entire thing for someone to have cut through it twice without anyone hearing the noise."

"You sure no one heard it or did they conveniently ignore it?" Smithson, the suit guy, looked at the house next to the lot with a sneer.

"No one around here is gonna ignore metal screeching, you idiot. And we didn't have any problems with the other storage, just *yours*."

The argument had everyone's attention, so Ruby carefully snuck under the tape and looked around the path leading up to the container. Nothing unusual, just dirt, rocks, and other stuff you'd expect to see around construction. Then the sun glinted off something shiny. Being careful, Ruby pulled it out of the dirt. A five- or six-inch piece of curved metal, bright red on one side and coppery red on the other. All of the edges were smooth, like it had been made by someone. For what, though?

"Hey kid!" one of the workers yelled. "It's dangerous to play over there!"

"Sorry!" she said, and ran back to her bike, keeping the metal hidden.

Before she rode away, Ruby saw the other side of the container. The hole was twice as big as the piece of metal the suit guy had been holding.

They'd mentioned two other burglary locations at the community meeting: the plumbing supply company and the Episcopal church. The first one was on the other side of Paddock Road and wasn't worth getting in trouble to visit if she got caught crossing over. The church was at the end of her street. It was starting to get dark, so she pedaled down there fast and hoped she'd find the stolen fence part easily.

She did. There was no missing the six-foot gap in

the wrought iron. "What the heck?" she said, walking up to where it had been cut. The deacon had said it looked sawed through—except the edges were smooth, almost melty. Ruby's mind flashed back to the hole in her window screen.

"Don't jump to conclusions," she said to herself. The markings looked similar, but there was no way a small bug could have done something like this. The fence parts were over two inches thick. According to the church folks, this all happened overnight.

Drag marks in the grass caught her attention. Something heavy had been pulled across the church lawn, so heavy that it dug up the grass to show the dirt below. Like a heavy iron fence. She followed the marks to the bushy, tree-crowded area behind the church's playground. It made a good hiding spot. The fence pieces weren't there, though, and the marks stopped just past the line of bushes. She did find one thing: A curly piece of metal that looked a little like a leaf. It was a topper from the fence—looking over at it again she saw them on all the remaining parts.

"They brought it back here and . . . what? Beamed it away?" She couldn't see any indication of someone going one way or the other. No footprints, no tire treads.

The streetlight on the block behind the trees clicked on. "Uh-oh." She hadn't realized how late it was. Ruby hopped back on her bike and sped home, hoping she wouldn't get any days added to her punishment.

CHAPTER EIGHT

On Friday after school Ruby was considering going back out to look for clues when Brandon came over and asked if she wanted to go to the store and then the playground with him and the others. She jumped up to get her bike before he could finish asking.

Once he got on his, Brandon pedaled through the neighbor's yard, cutting over to the side street. The one that ran past Witchypoo's house.

"Uh-uh. I don't need those dogs chasing me," she said, squeezing her brakes.

"They won't."

"You psychic now?" Ruby said. They couldn't see the dogs right then, but that didn't mean anything. The dogs often hid in the bushes, so it was hard to tell when they were out.

"No one has seen them for a week," he said, and pushed off again. "Ever since the day those men showed up."

Ruby followed, keeping an eye on Witchypoo's backyard just in case. "What happened to them?"

"Don't know, don't care. Maybe they took them away for growling like maniacs."

When they met up with Hollie and the others, Ruby's friends all said the same: They hadn't seen the dogs in days. And they were all more relieved than curious.

"Someone probably called animal control, finally," Hollie pronounced. "Or maybe one of the dogs bit those government men and they impounded them. White people don't play."

They looked to Mayson and she nodded. "It's true, we don't." They all laughed.

Ruby didn't think the dogs had been taken away. If the G-men had done it, she hadn't seen them, and she'd been watching them the whole time they were on the block. If they had come back the next day, people would have noticed.

When they had to go home for dinner she and Hollie rode together past Witchypoo's house—still no sign of the dogs. It was nice to not have to go all the way down the other end of the block to get home, but Ruby couldn't help but wonder what had happened to the dogs and whether it had something to do with everything else going on. Then she saw something that made her brake hard.

A piece of black metal was lying in Witchypoo's side yard. Curled, flat metal like the swirly decorations on top of the church fence. Inching closer (because she was still afraid the dogs might appear), Ruby stared and stared until she was sure. *What is that doing* here? she wondered.

"Ruby!" Gramma called from the kitchen door. "Get in here and wash your hands."

"Yes ma'am," she said, pulling herself away. This definitely warranted more observation.

After dinner she went straight up to her bedroom where she had a good view of the side of Witchypoo's house. Not that it did much good seeing how overgrown the plants were. That night she watched to see if any lights came on—none did, but she didn't know if that meant anything. *Had she ever seen lights on at Witchypoo's?* Could be the old woman's bedroom was on the back of the house. She needed to get a closer look.

The next morning Ruby searched through the upstairs

closet and found her daddy's binoculars. They were big and powerful enough to see Jupiter on a clear night; perfect for looking into a window a few yards away. Of course she knew that peeping on the neighbors was not okay under normal circumstances. This was an emergency, she told herself. A potential emergency, anyway.

It ended up not mattering. Even with the binoculars she couldn't see in the windows. They were too covered with vines and dirt. No matter how long she looked she couldn't tell if anyone was moving around.

"Now what?" she asked herself. The only thing she could think was to go look at the back of the house. It was visible from the street they always avoided. She went out and stood on the sidewalk, trying to see past the glare of the sun. Those windows were less dirty and she probably could have seen into them if she were up higher. No chance of that. The building behind Witchypoo's house was a business, and it didn't have windows on the second floor even if she could figure out a way to get in there.

Maybe the binoculars might work from down on the street, except . . .

"Hey Ruby," Miz Ella said. She lived in the house behind their next-door neighbor and was working in her garden. "Be careful, them dogs might be out."

"No one's seen them in a week."

Miz Ella frowned and looked across at the overgrown backyard. "Huh. I guess she got spooked by those men. I heard her yelling at them that day. Whatever makes her keep them inside." She went back to gardening.

Unless the "whatever" was something or someone dangerous, Ruby thought. From her observations, the thieves making off with stuff around the neighborhood were doing it quickly and quietly and had a way to get into secure areas using some weird metal cutter. She couldn't figure out why they were stealing car parts and pipes and fences, she just knew there had to be a reason. How did this fit in with the weird bug? That was still fuzzy.

However, looking over at the piece of iron in Witchypoo's yard again, Ruby felt confident making a hypothesis: Whoever was responsible for all this had a connection to the old lady. And since she didn't like people and never let anyone in the house, no one would think to look for them there.

The folks who lived around the block usually kept an eye on things. If Miz Ella or Alberto's papi weren't out in their gardens, Mrs. Tidmore or Miz Barnfield or her gramma would be sitting on their porches. Wesley who did everyone's lawns and walked their dogs saw everything that went on. And what he didn't see, he heard about from Brandon's brothers who shot hoops in their driveway most afternoons. That's why Ruby and the other kids could be, as her mama put it, free-range children.

As much attention as everyone paid to everything going on, that's how much attention they *didn't* pay to Witchypoo's house. It was like the old woman had made herself so unlikable the house became a black hole. You could observe things around it, not inside it, and everyone was fine with that.

Ruby thought of something else: if some gang of thieves or whatever was hiding in Witchypoo's house, she probably hadn't let them in on purpose.

No matter how much she wanted to find out the truth, standing in the street with binoculars wasn't an option. Especially if she didn't have a good explanation.

Then it hit her: The drone. Her uncle Buddy had gotten her a drone for her birthday and it had a camera on it. She could fly it up to Witchypoo's back windows and see inside. All she needed was a tablet or smartphone to control it.

She could use her own if she waited another three weeks. Or, she could get help now.

CHAPTER NINE

After church the next day Ruby went down to Hollie's house. She and her brothers were hanging out on the porch. Frankie Lee, the older one, was on the phone talking to someone. A girl, by the sound of his voice. He was fourteen and allowed to go on dates, something Gramma complained about every time she saw him walking down the street holding hands with someone.

"'Sup cuz?" he said, giving Ruby a fist bump before going back to his conversation.

Hollie was playing a handheld game while her baby brother, Courtney, watched over her shoulder.

"Hey, can I talk to you?" Ruby asked. "It's important."

"Certainly." Hollie didn't even have to ask if she meant in private.

She handed the game to Courtney, who whined. "But you said you'd show me how to get past the boss."

"I just did! You need to practice," she said, leaving to go up to her room with Ruby. Courtney tried to follow.

"This is a private conversation," Ruby said.

"I'm your cousin! No secrets from cousins." He was seven and already as much of a pain as Brandon.

"Ugh, you don't have to be part of every conversation we have!" Hollie said.

Ruby knew how to handle this. "Hollie, I think I'm having my first period and I need girl advice!" she practically shouted.

"EW!"

They laughed as he ran back down the stairs. Boys were so easy.

"So what did you really wanna talk about?" Hollie asked when they were in her room behind a locked door.

"This is going to sound nuts . . ." She told Hollie about how she suspected the dogs going missing had something to do with the thefts, and how maybe criminals were hiding out in Witchypoo's house, and how she needed a tablet to investigate further. After she was done Hollie stared at her for a good minute.

"You right, that sounds nuts. No."

"Come ON," Ruby whined. "I just want to make sure Witchypoo is safe and not . . . I dunno, being held hostage."

"People only get held hostage on TV."

"Yeah, on the TV news!" Ruby frowned at the disbelieving look on Hollie's face. "It can't hurt to just look and make sure."

"It'll hurt if we get caught. You best believe Witchypoo will call the cops on us." Hollie crossed her arms and that was almost the end of it. Then she looked like a thought had occurred to her. "If she's not letting the dogs out, though . . . that might mean she's hurt or something. Mama says she has no family. And she won't let anyone in."

"Yeah, exactly! What if it's like that commercial where old people fall down and they can't get to the phone?"

"Uuuuuuuuuuugggghhhh." Hollie groaned. "Okay, okay! I'll help only because Witchypoo might need help. But we need a plan. If we fly that thing around when someone is looking they're gonna get mad no matter how altruistic we're being."

Ruby rolled her eyes. "You and your big words."

"You want my help or not?" She smiled, though,

and went to get her school tablet. "I have to download an app first, right?"

"First you have to jailbreak it so you can install unapproved apps." Ruby went to take the tablet from her but Hollie yanked it out of reach.

"You're not allowed to use it unsupervised!"

"Oh, come on, Hollie! We're alone, my parents ain't gonna find out."

"Nope. You tell me how to do it."

She was such a rule follower. Well, one of them had to be, Ruby figured. They settled on the bed and got to work.

🕷 🕷 🕷

They spent the afternoon getting the drone and the tablet connected, which required going back to Ruby's house and hiding what they were doing from her parents. Once they got it working Ruby was ready to try it out right away. Hollie had to pull her up short.

"We'll get caught for sure if we do it when everyone can see us."

"If we stand in my backyard the only people we really have to worry about are Miz Ella and Gramma," Ruby said. "If we put the drone across the street instead of flying it from here then no one else will see it."

"You are way too devious."

"No, I'm too smart for my own good. Just ask Gramma."

She hadn't said so in a couple of years, not since Mama complained that her saying it might "undermine Ruby's self-esteem" and make her not want to be smart. So now Gramma just said it with her eyes.

Together they determined that 5:30 the next day was the best time since anyone who might see them would be busy making dinner.

Right on time Hollie showed up at Ruby's house, tablet hidden in her backpack, and they claimed to be going out to play until food was ready.

"Just don't get all dirty," Gramma said after them.

"Why does she always say that?" Ruby whispered.

"Because you always digging in dirt looking for bugs," Hollie whispered back.

"*That* is a stereotype." She got the drone out from where she'd hidden it earlier. Looking around to be sure no one was watching, she ran it across the street, set it up near Witchypoo's backyard, then ran back.

"Okay, the app says it's connected. What do I press to turn the camera on?" Hollie asked.

"That button. I should fly it, I know how."

"You're not allowed!"

“Shhh!!!” Ruby glanced over to make sure Gramma hadn’t heard.

“Just watch the video feed and I’ll watch the drone.”

Watching Hollie clumsily work the controls made Ruby itch to take the tablet from her. They probably should have practiced just flying it around before they attempted this. Too late now. The drone lifted off the ground, wobbled, dipped, almost crashed, swooped up, then finally leveled off, all while Ruby kept saying “Careful!” and Hollie kept saying “I got it, I got it, stop freaking out!” She flew the drone up to the second-story windows of Witchypoo’s house and Ruby crowded closer to see the video feed. As she thought, the windows weren’t as dirty there and once the drone got close enough, she could finally see a room inside. It was filled with boxes and junk, probably used as storage.

“Go to the next one. Left.”

The drone drifted over and shook a bunch as Hollie tried to steady it. Once it did and Ruby saw what was on the video feed, she screamed.

CHAPTER TEN

The bug. The bug that Ruby had found and that the G-men had supposedly taken away. It was *not* away. *It was in Witchypoo's room.*

Hollie jerked away from her. "Ow! What!" Then she saw the video. "WHAT THE—!"

The bug was bigger than it had been. Much, much bigger. The size of one of Witchypoo's dogs. And it was standing ON WITCHYPOO, who was lying on the bed.

Both of them freaked all the way out. Hollie accidentally swiped the controls and the drone went zooming away from the house—

"No, go back, go back!" Ruby shouted.

—and careened right into the window of the building behind it.

The video feed stopped.

The two of them stared open-mouthed at the drone, now lying broken on the ground, and the huge crack in the window it had made.

"Oh no," Ruby said.

"We are *so* in trouble," Hollie answered.

Gramma came out the side door. "What are y'all out here yelling about?"

Before they could come up with a lie, Mr. Bell, the man who owned the business behind Witchypoo's house, came out the back door and started cursing. "My window!"

"Big, big trouble," Ruby said.

🕷 🕷 🕷

Ruby and Hollie had been banished and confined to the living room where they had to "sit quietly until your parents get home" or else face the further wrath of Gramma. They were lucky—she was only mad at them for breaking Mr. Bell's window and being irresponsible with their toys. Even as freaked out as they were, neither girl was going to tell her what they'd really been doing as it would put them in even more trouble. Hollie had almost talked herself out of the idea that she'd seen what she saw.

"That was a trick, right? You tricked me. You did

something with AR," Hollie anger-whispered. They weren't supposed to be talking.

"No! Hollie, that thing was really there. I'm not lying!"

"But it was huge. You said it was small like a . . . a spider."

That part still made Ruby's stomach twist in knots. "It was when I caught it. How did it get so big so fast?"

"Maybe it's not the same one. There's a bigger one, like a mama bug. Oh God . . ." The very thought made Hollie start to breathe too fast.

"We gotta do something," Ruby kept saying. She had no idea what *to* do. "We gotta tell someone."

"They won't believe us! They'll think we're making it up to get out of trouble." This was, unfortunately, a common tactic in Hollie's house. Frankie Lee made up all kinds of wild stories when he got caught doing stuff. No matter how many times Gramma brought up the Boy Who Cried Wolf, he kept on at it. And it was rubbing off on Courtney. Hollie had distinguished herself as the one child who did not tell lies. At least not obvious ones her parents found out about.

"They'll believe *you*," Ruby said.

"Not if I tell them a giant spider thing is living in Witchypoo's house. Not without proof."

Proof they didn't have. The camera on the drone had streamed the video, but Ruby had forgotten to turn on the recording in the app.

"We can't just let it stay in there. What if it comes out and—" Finishing that sentence made Ruby freaked out all over again. All she could think about was seeing the bug standing on top of Witchypoo. This was the first time she'd ever regretted making a scientific observation. The more Ruby thought back, the more she remembered. Like how Witchypoo's body had been covered in this weblike stuff that reminded her of bugs trapped in a spiderweb. What if it was feasting on her a little at a time? Or even worse, like a parasitic wasp that lays eggs inside and the larvae eat their way out? These thoughts were so upsetting Ruby started to cry.

Hollie hugged her close. "It's gonna be all right. We'll do something. We can . . . we can . . ." She struggled for a minute, and then: "We can get someone to do a wellness check!"

"A what?"

"My mama sometimes calls them in. It's when you think a person might be hurt because they haven't answered the phone or door. Like older people who live alone."

Ruby wiped her cheeks and sniffed. "Who'll come

to check on her? The police?" She didn't want anything worse to happen.

"No, it'll be someone from Bond Hill CCP and maybe an ambulance."

This did seem like a better plan. The people from the Community Care Program were trained to help people but didn't carry guns. Maybe that would be good enough. The only other people she thought they could call were those men from the government. And she had no idea how to do that. Not like they left a card. "How do we get a wellness check?"

"Mama usually calls the non-emergency number. I know exactly what to say, too." Hollie put on her grown-up-white-lady voice. "No one has seen our neighbor for over a week. Her dogs have been inside and barking nonstop for days. She won't answer the door. We're very concerned because she has no family in the area."

"No one would knock on her door." That's when Ruby realized she hadn't heard the dogs barking even though they probably should be if they hadn't been let out.

"Yeah but *they* don't know that. You have to say the right things to get them to check."

"We should call right now."

At that moment, they heard Daddy and Hollie's mom, Peggy, come into the kitchen through the side door.

"Mama, your text made no sense. What is going on?" Aunt Peggy said to Gramma.

"They rammed this into Mr. Bell's window." Gramma waved the mangled drone at their parents.

"We didn't!" Ruby couldn't help but say. Hollie muttered for her to hush.

"Then how did the window get that crack? Magic?"

"Hollie Ann Rembert, you better have a good explanation." Aunt Peggy had gone right to middle names. That was never a good sign.

"We didn't ram it on purpose. We were flying it and it went all crazy out of control! I was trying to bring it down and it just flew across the street!" Hollie didn't get in trouble hardly ever. When she did, she was ready to talk her way out of it.

"It 'just flew' huh?" Daddy was skeptical.

"I think there was some interference because of all the Wi-Fi signals," Ruby said.

"And isn't that why I told you to only fly this thing in the park?"

"Oh right," she said, sinking down. "You did say that. I forgot."

"I didn't know." Hollie jumped in. "If I had I wouldn't have asked her to show me, Uncle Jimmy. I swear."

Ruby's mama came in then and the whole thing had

to be explained again. She gave both girls an exasperated look, then shook her head. "I told Buddy not to buy her that thing in the first place."

"We're really sorry," Hollie said, and Ruby echoed her.

"Since it was an accident, we'll accept that. But the window is still broken." Aunt Peggy looked to her sister. "No allowance until the damage is paid off?"

"That sounds reasonable to me," Mama said.

"I'll find out how much it'll be." Daddy went back outside to talk to Mr. Bell.

The loss of what would probably be a month's allowance would have upset Ruby except she was more worried about the giant red bug hanging out a few houses down.

"Come on, your dad says dinner is ready." Aunt Peggy gathered up Hollie and kissed Ruby on the forehead before heading out. As they walked through the door Hollie mouthed, *I'll call from home*.

Mama sat down beside Ruby. "I can tell you really are sorry," she said, wiping a stray tear from Ruby's jaw. "And so I won't bring up to Daddy that I know you need a tablet or a smartphone to fly that drone."

"I didn't touch the tablet, I swear! Hollie wouldn't let me."

"I'm sure that's true. And yet, we have talked about

the spirit of the law versus the letter of the law, haven't we?"

"Yes," she mumbled.

Mama pulled her into a hug. "Then I'll leave it at that."

Ruby considered telling her about the bug. She and Hollie weren't in big trouble, so there was no reason for Mama to think the story was a lie. There was still the part about no proof, though. And she did not want her parents to think she was starting to be like Frankie Lee and making up elaborate stories. Waiting until the people from the Bond Hill Community Cares Program came to check on Witchypoo was better, because then it would be adults talking about it.

Assuming they would come. Hollie could pass for a grown-up on the phone sometimes, but would the operator believe it? How long would it take for someone to show up?

If they didn't come by bedtime, Ruby decided, she'd tell her parents everything.

CHAPTER ELEVEN

Neither of Ruby's parents were as mad as Gramma had been. All through dinner she talked about how, in her day, people didn't give kids expensive toys that could fly around for miles and crash through people's windows. Never mind that this was not even close to what the drone could or did do, she was determined to be in a huff about it. Ruby barely heard any of this because she was listening for sirens and looking in the kitchen to see if the cabinets were reflecting red flashing lights. Nothing yet.

She ate fast and asked if she could go to her room—there she had a better view of Witchypoo's house. Other than waiting on the BHCCP she wasn't sure why she felt like she needed to keep watch. Even if the bug did come out, what would she do? Chase it? Tell her parents to chase it?

It was over two hours from when Hollie left before an ambulance and a car finally pulled up on the block. The man who got out of the car was Mr. Harshaw, the director of the CCP for their neighborhood. Daddy trusted him and Ruby liked him, so she didn't like seeing him go up to Witchypoo's door. What if the bug attacked?

A white man she didn't recognize got out of the ambulance, went up the front steps behind Mr. Harshaw, and disappeared behind the bushes. After some knocking and calling out, there was a big crash—Ruby assumed it was them knocking down the door. Her stomach twisted and turned as she listened for the sound of a struggle or yelling or something. She kept looking over at the clock. Two minutes . . . five . . . eight . . . the quiet stretched on forever. If they didn't come out, would that mean the bug had gotten them, too? If it ate them, would calling the police help? Would they have a chance before the bug came out and attacked other people on the block? Ruby felt scared and helpless and couldn't stop imagining the worst.

Then something she didn't expect: The man from the ambulance ran back out of the house yelling to his partner to get the stretcher. They went in with it and, forever later, they came back out with Witchypoo on it! Not all covered up, like when someone is dead, but with a mask over her face giving oxygen.

"She's alive!" Ruby yelled, half relieved, half surprised. The bug hadn't eaten her after all. Or maybe it hadn't had time to eat all of her.

Back when the ambulance arrived people had started coming out on their porches to see what was going on. When they saw Witchypoo on a stretcher, they crossed the street to find out more. Ruby even spotted her daddy walking up to Mr. Harshaw and talking to him. No one seemed freaked out. No one was acting like they'd seen a dog-sized bug in the house. Had it run away?

Worried, Ruby went out to try to pull Daddy toward home, just in case the bug was waiting for more victims or its babies started bursting out of Witchypoo. As she ran up, she overheard Mr. Harshaw say that animal control was coming for the dogs.

"They were closed up in the kitchen. Who knows for how long? One of 'em looks pretty bad."

"Damn. It's a good thing y'all went in there," Daddy said.

Ruby wrapped her arms around his waist. "Is Witchypoo gonna be okay?"

"Mrs. Reed should be fine once she gets to a hospital," Mr. Harshaw said.

"Mrs. Reed??"

"Yes, that is her name."

She hadn't ever heard anyone say her real name. Even the adults called her Witchypoo.

"Let me know if we can help out finding her family," Daddy said and gave him a fist bump.

"Will do. Thanks, man."

Ruby gently tugged at Daddy's arm until he started walking back to the house. "It's safer inside."

"Safe from what?"

A giant, person-eating bug. "The dogs. What if they get out? And are mad? And start chasing and biting everyone?"

"You are an alarmist, my little love."

Whatever that meant she would own it, as long as her daddy went back inside.

* * *

It was pretty late when the activity on the block calmed down and Mama insisted Ruby go up to bed. She got in her jammies and turned out the light. She did not go to sleep. There was too much to think about and besides, the bug was still out there somewhere. The EMTs hadn't found it—if they had they wouldn't have let people stand around on the sidewalk. And those G-men hadn't shown up. So where did it go? Was it still hiding in the house? Or did it run away? As big as it was now, the bushes and weeds and stuff around Witchypoo's house were still thick enough for it to sneak out unseen. The dogs had hidden in there well. If it was hiding, it was smart enough to avoid everyone who went inside.

That thought kept her up and staring out the window at Witchypoo's for a long time.

At around one in the morning, when her eyes were starting to droop, Ruby figured she should go to bed for real. Then she saw something, or thought she did, in the trees behind the house. The binoculars were still in her room and she grabbed them fast to get a closer look. Just when she raised them up there was a flash of light, then another, then more, sort of like a strobe light going off. Then a dark shape shot straight into the sky. It was hard to make out, and she blinked a bunch of times trying to see it better. Before she could, the thing flew away so fast it didn't seem real.

"I'm not dreaming. I'm not." She pinched herself because that's what you're supposed to do when you think you're dreaming, or so she'd heard. The pinch did hurt, so she was awake. Wasn't she?

Looking toward the backyard with the binoculars again she didn't see the light or anything else. It was dark and quiet on the street like it should be.

Did I imagine it? Ruby wondered. *No,* she decided. *That was real. A real thing that happened.*

That must have been the bug and, if it was, then it meant the thing could fly. Now there was a war going on in her brain. One part of Ruby—the scientist part—wanted to know how it flew so high and how it got so big so fast and why it had been in Witchypoo's house and what it had done to her. The other part of her was terrified of a giant, experimental bug that feasted slowly on humans and could go anywhere it wanted. She decided that it flying away was good. Where did it go, though? Did it leave the neighborhood entirely? She tried to convince herself of that. Tried very hard.

But Ruby got no rest that night.

CHAPTER TWELVE

The next morning on the bus all the kids from the block were talking about the drama at Witchypoo's house. One kid was sure she'd been found doing witch rituals in the basement and another said that the Devil himself had come for her, then had a shootout with the police. Ruby was too exhausted to join in, even to correct all the stupid stories about what happened. She and Hollie sat together near the back, neither saying much.

"You sure they didn't find it?" Hollie said in a low voice so the others wouldn't hear.

Ruby shook her head. "None of the EMTs said anything about it." There hadn't been anything on the news about an old woman in the hospital exploding into a hundred tiny bugs, so she guessed that at least they didn't have to worry about that part.

Hollie sank down lower in the seat. "Great. I had nightmares about that thing all night."

Now Ruby wondered if she should tell her about seeing something fly away. Would it make her feel better? It seemed to her it would just upset Hollie more, and she was upset enough.

Between her lack of sleep and still being freaked out by what she had seen, Ruby went through the day like a zombie. She didn't raise her hand once in any of her classes, barely spoke, and couldn't remember what the teachers had said five minutes after they said it. In science class she started to drift into microsleeps, and each time she did the giant red bug was there in her mind, coming after her, bigger and bigger, until she jumped awake.

"Ruby!" Mrs. Bailey yelled, which startled her out of a dream so abruptly she fell off her chair. All the other kids laughed—Brandon the loudest.

"Quiet!" the teacher said to the others as she came to help her up. "Are you okay?"

"Yeah, sorry," Ruby mumbled.

"Let's have a chat outside," Mrs. Bailey said. "The rest of you, finish your worksheets. Without talking."

"You in trouuuuuuuuble," Brandon singsonged under his breath. She was too exhausted and embarrassed to bother giving him a nasty look.

Out in the hall, Mrs. Bailey sat her down on a bench. "You've been pretty out of it all class. Is something wrong?"

"I didn't get a lot of sleep last night. One of my neighbors got taken away in an ambulance," Ruby said.

"And you're worried about her?"

"Yeah." That was close enough to the truth. Not like Mrs. Bailey would believe her if she said she was worried about a dog-sized insect terrorizing the neighborhood.

"Is there anything else going on keeping you from sleeping? Something with your parents?"

Ruby blinked at her. "My parents? Why would my parents keep me awake?"

"I'm sure they don't mean to. Sometimes it happens, if you're worried about them or if they're fighting or—"

"They aren't fighting." *Why is she saying such weird things?* Ruby wondered.

"Okay. That's good," Mrs. Bailey said, smiling in an odd way. Ruby hoped she could exit this conversation now, but instead: "Have you decided on a new science fair project yet? The deadline for getting your proposal approved is less than two weeks away."

"I'm gonna stick with the experiment I submitted before."

"Ruby, I thought we decided you would choose a new one from the list."

"I said I would consider it, and I did, and I don't want to do one of those other projects." She didn't like the way Mrs. Bailey was looking at her now, blue eyes narrowed and mouth all pinched in a frown. No way was she going to back down, though.

"Then you can't take part in the science fair."

"What!"

Mrs. Bailey crossed her arms. "I won't approve an unrealistic project that won't reflect well on the school or on me as your teacher."

"I don't need you to," Ruby said, standing up straighter and crossing her own arms.

"Excuse me?"

"I can get my project approved by the district Science Council. It's in the rules." Ruby's tone was sliding into the disrespectful, and if she'd been less tired and out of cares to give she would have checked herself. She didn't. "And my old science teacher said he would help me, so I don't have to get approval from you."

Her teacher took several breaths before speaking again. "You're being extremely rude right now."

"You're being mean telling me I can't do my project!"

"That's it. Get your backpack and go to the principal's office. Now."

"Fine!" Ruby knew she shouldn't be yelling at an adult, or stomping as she got her bag, or shooting Mrs. Bailey a dirty look. She didn't care anymore.

But once she walked into the office she cared a little. She didn't usually get in the kind of trouble that landed kids in here. Teachers and principals liked her because she was smart and got good grades. Would the principal think she was a bad kid now? That upset her.

The office administrator, Mr. Segal, was on the in-school phone when she walked in. "Yes, she's here now. Okay."

Ruby usually liked seeing him because he made her laugh. He was a tall white man—so tall he towered over most of the teachers. He would tease all the kids by asking for high fives then put his arm way up.

He didn't offer a high five now, but he did smile sympathetically once he hung up the phone. "Bad day?"

Ruby nodded. "Mrs. Bailey said I had to come here."

"She did. However, the principal is in a meeting. Would you like to talk to Miss Valya, the school counselor, instead?"

"I can do that?"

"Oh yeah." He winked. "Come with me."

They walked to the next office down where Miss Valya was sitting at her computer. Ruby had seen her the first week of school—a slight white woman with long, pretty brown hair and a friendly smile, which she gave when they came in.

"This is Ruby Finley. She's having a little trouble today, think you can talk to her?" Mr. Segal said.

"Of course. Have a seat." After Miss Valya got her a cup of water she came from behind her desk and sat next to Ruby. "Want to tell me what happened?"

Once Ruby started talking it all came out in a rush. "There's some weird stuff going on in my neighborhood and last night one of my neighbors was taken away in an ambulance and I didn't sleep and today is terrible and then, I didn't mean to, but I was disrespectful to Mrs. Bailey because she said she wouldn't approve my science fair project because it's too ambitious for me but I worked really hard on it already and I want to get a high score and I don't know why she won't let me."

"That . . . is quite a bit of stuff to have going on," she said. "Also understandable. When people don't get enough sleep they do things they wouldn't normally do, like snap at others."

The counselor asked her more questions in a kind

way. The longer they talked, the more Ruby wanted to tell her about what was really bothering her: the bug. There was no way Miss Valya would believe her about it, so there was no point mentioning it, but it was at the heart of everything. Miss Valya even commented at one point that Ruby seemed to be holding something back, to which she could only shrug.

"It's okay not to talk about everything today. Or to not talk to me about it. You should talk to someone, though. Do you feel like your parents listen to you?"

"Yeah, they do. And Mama says I can talk to them about anything, even if it's scary or upsetting."

"That's good!" Miss Valya said, smiling. "And if you feel like it, you can talk to me, too. About anything."

After that conversation Ruby realized she did need to talk to someone about this bug situation. Getting it out would make her feel better. Adults might not believe her if she told them, but she knew people who would.

CHAPTER THIRTEEN

"We need to tell Jackie and them about the bug," Ruby told Hollie on the bus home.

"Why?" She didn't look much better than Ruby felt and must have had a hard day, too.

"Because we need to talk about it or else we're gonna have nightmares forever. And maybe they can help us figure out what to do."

Hollie looked skeptical. "I don't know . . ."

"We can't keep this bottled up. Miss Valya said that's not healthy."

"You told her?!"

"Not about the bug." Ruby whispered the last word.

"Good. I don't need people thinking we're having hallucinations." Hollie looked over at where Brandon and Alberto were sneakily eating the former's homemade baklava. "Maybe you're right, we should tell them."

"We'll all figure it out together."

They had to wait awhile before everyone could come out. Mayson got home later than the rest of them since her school was all the way downtown, and Alberto and Jackie couldn't leave their houses until they finished all their homework. The wait felt like forever. Ruby was too distracted to do her own homework and she couldn't pass the time playing on her xCUBE. Finally, Hollie and Jackie knocked on the door and she shot out to get her bike with barely a word to Gramma of where they were going.

Over at the playground, Brandon and Mayson were on the swings trying to see who could jump the farthest and Alberto was perched at the top of the monkey bars.

"What's up?" he called down when they rolled over. "You made it sound serious."

"It is," Ruby said. She glanced at Hollie, who nodded for her to go on, then she told them all the story. The whole story. Except for the part about what she saw in the middle of the night. She needed them to believe and that seemed a step too far.

Once she was done she looked at the others, waiting for their reaction.

"Y'all lyin,'" Brandon said, and threw his hand at them.

"We are not! Unlike you, I don't make a habit of lying," Hollie said.

"But it can't be true," Alberto said, coming down from the bars. "There's no way some giant insect was hanging out in Witchypoo's house for a week and she didn't notice!"

"Who said she didn't notice? That crazy old woman probably invited it in. Remember how she didn't want those government men near her house?" Jackie said.

"I don't think so," Ruby said. "I think the bug did something to her. When we saw it through the window she was lying on the bed and had this . . . this webbing all over her." Ruby felt sick to her stomach remembering it. "She didn't have that stuff on her when they brought her out, so the bug must have taken it off."

"Webbing? Like a spider?" Now Alberto paced around, freaked out. "The kind spiders wrap around the bugs they're going to eat?"

"Trust me, you don't wanna think too hard about that," Hollie said, and Ruby knew she'd been dwelling on it, too.

"Y'all, don't listen to them!" Brandon jumped off the swing. "They're just trying to scare us. If there'd been some big ol' insect in that house the EMTs and Mr. Harshaw would have seen it."

"Not if it hid from them." Mayson had been quiet up to now. "My mom says that bug is some experiment that escaped from the government."

This was usually when they'd all start teasing her about her mom's conspiracy talk. Not this time.

"If they made it, maybe they made it really smart so it could think and hide," Mayson suggested. "You said she didn't have the web stuff on her when they came to get her, and it probably knows you saw it with the drone. It covered its tracks."

That was a very, very, very unpleasant thought.

"Not y'all listening to *her*! There's no way!" Brandon saw he was in the minority on this one. "How do you explain how it got as big as you say?"

"I can't!" Ruby said. "All I know is that when I caught it, the bug fit in a mason jar and when I saw it through Witchypoo's window it looked as big as her dogs."

"And Mr. Harshaw didn't notice something that size?"

"Maybe he didn't search the house," Jackie said, stepping to Brandon. "They went in there to do a wellness check on Witchypoo and found her. Why look around? They knew she lived alone."

"And if the bug is really smart then it would have hidden somewhere they weren't likely to go," Mayson said. All of them were quiet for a minute.

Alberto, who was still pacing around in a circle, stopped short. "If we knew what Mr. Harshaw saw when they went in the house we could figure it out, I bet. Maybe it left clues that Harshaw didn't realize were clues."

"Oh come on, man," Brandon said, exasperated. "You been watching too many mystery shows with your grandad."

Ruby ignored him. "How do we find out what they saw in there? I don't think he'll just tell us if we ask."

"You have to ask the right way," Jackie said. "Trick him into giving you the information you want." When they all looked at her, surprised, she shrugged. "My gramma watches mystery shows, too."

A few minutes later they were all riding their bikes down the street, a plan in place. They headed toward the Bond Hill Community Cares Program—a small store-front in their neighborhood used as a base. Like usual, Mr. Harshaw was inside with a small number of staffers.

"All right, Brandon, you start," Jackie said before they went in. "And do like I told you."

"Hey y'all," Mr. Harshaw said when he saw them. "Something wrong?"

"Nah, I was just telling them how you found a whole bunch of dead animals in Witchypoo's house last night and they don't believe me," Brandon said.

"You mean Mrs. Reed?" Mr. Harshaw said.

"Who?"

"That's her real name, duh," Ruby cut in. "But I bet she was a real witch and had a . . . a pentagram on her floor so she could call the Devil."

Jackie made a big show of rolling her eyes. "Can you please, please tell these fools they're wrong? They been arguing about this for an hour."

Mrs. Riley, the light-skinned woman who was in charge of homeless outreach, chuckled. "I told you the rumors were gonna fly."

Harshaw sighed and came around the desk to talk to them. "I know people have said a lot of wild stuff about Mrs. Reed and what she did in that house. However, it's all unfounded. She is not a witch."

"Then how do you explain all the dead animals!!" Brandon said, overplaying his role, in Ruby's opinion.

"There were no dead animals. Even the dogs were alive. Mad, but alive."

"You sure you saw the whole house?" Ruby asked. "Maybe she kept her witch stuff in the basement."

He shook his head. "Nope. No witch stuff. But . . ." He paused and looked like he was considering something before he kept talking. "Look, we did notice that some of her stuff might be missing."

It worked! Ruby thought. "Might be?"

"There were no forks or spoons or any flatware in her kitchen, no pots and pans either. And there was a hole in the wall of her living room where it looks like someone tried to get at some wiring. We think maybe someone was in that house who wasn't her. But she's still in the hospital and still in a coma, so we won't know until she gets better."

They all stared at him. What the heck was going on?

"Have any of you seen anyone going in and out of that house but her? Or just someone hanging around near her yard?" Harshaw asked.

"No," Ruby said. "People don't go over there."

Hollie and the others nodded. "Yeah, she always yelled at anyone who tried. Except the mailwoman and Jackson from the store who delivers her groceries to the porch."

"My papi says she acted the way she did to make sure people left her alone," Alberto added.

"She did, that's true." Mr. Harshaw looked thoughtful. "She's lucky at least one person noticed that something was wrong. Anyway, if you do see someone around her yard who doesn't look official, promise me you'll tell someone here or your parents."

"We will," Jackie answered.

"Good. Now, no more of this witch talk. Things are hard enough for her without people thinking she's messin' with the Devil. Okay?"

"Okay," they all echoed before walking out and riding back to the playground on their bikes. No one talked for a full five minutes. All of them were trying to absorb what they heard.

Ruby kept going over and over it in her head. *Stick to the method, what do you know?*

"Let's look at this scientifically," she said, breaking the silence.

"Oh here she goes," Brandon started.

Ruby spoke over him. "The silverware, pots, and pans were missing from Witchypoo's house. The bug had tried to get at wires. And remember all those thefts last week? What went missing? Pipes, copper building materials, iron fence pieces, car parts."

"Metal," Hollie said. "That bug is collecting metal!"

"Why, though? That's what I can't figure out."

"Maybe it needs metal to do something or . . . or build something," Mayson said.

Ruby nodded. "On top of that, it's getting bigger. When it was small it cut or burned or whatever through glass and metal. How much more damage is it gonna do as it grows?"

Alberto waved his hands to stop them. "Okay. Okay. Say . . . say all of this is true. Say it really is some government experiment capable of hiding and covering its tracks—"

"Seriously?" Brandon interjected.

"That means it's not still in that house," Alberto went on, ignoring him. "Right? It must know that people are gonna be up in there at some point, even if Witchypoo—Mrs. Reed—doesn't come back right away. It's not safe there, anymore. That means it probably left."

Ruby thought back to the night before. "I did see—I thought I saw—something flying away out of Witchypoo's yard in the middle of the night. I *think*. I was so tired . . ."

Hollie reacted just as she thought she would. "You really need to stop leaving out crucial details, Ruby!"

"So it's gone." Alberto jumped on the idea. "It flew away. Meaning we don't have to worry about it."

"Uh . . . I'm still very worried," Hollie said.

"He's right, though," Jackie said. "I know y'all are freaked out and I would be, too, if I saw what you saw. It's still out there somewhere but it sure ain't hanging around here."

"And so it's someone else's problem. Not that it's even real." Brandon was sticking to his stubborn denial. Ruby rolled her eyes at him.

"We should try to warn people." Mayson's gaze was on the ground and her voice was quiet. "If it's gone from here then it'll find some other house and some other person to wrap up."

"We have no proof. We don't even have video from the drone," Hollie said. "No one's gonna believe us."

Mayson crossed her arms and looked defensive the way she always did when she started saying the kind of stuff her mom would say. "I know some places online where they will."

Brandon was about to say something. No doubt it was gonna be mean. Jackie got right in his face. "Don't. Even. Say it. Let her talk." Since she was a good six inches taller and could beat him up without breaking a sweat, he backed down.

"My mom spends a lot of time in Facebook groups and Discord servers where they talk about stuff like this—secret government cover-ups and weird things that happen. I know how to access them." She looked around to see if any of them were going to make fun of her like they usually did. No one was laughing.

Hollie went over and put an arm around her. "That's actually a good idea. At least then someone out there will know."

Ruby, Alberto, and Jackie agreed. None of them cared about what Brandon was muttering under his breath.

"You post the story and tell us what the people there say. Maybe we're not alone and there are more than one of those bugs out there," Hollie said.

"That absolutely doesn't make me feel any better," Alberto said.

"Y'all getting worked up over something that ain't even real. I'm out." Brandon grabbed his bike and pedaled away.

"Who cares about you, then!" Ruby shouted at his back. She smiled in satisfaction when his response—the middle finger—almost made him lose his balance on his bike.

CHAPTER FOURTEEN

Despite what Alberto and Jackie said, Ruby kept an eye on Witchypoo's, just in case. In the afternoons she poked around in the backyard to see if she could spot the place where the bug had taken off. If she could find scorch marks or something she could ask Mayson to post pictures of it to Miz Trish's groups. More data was always better. She could never get deep enough to find anything; an adult always called her away, saying it might be dangerous.

Witchypoo being taken off in an ambulance hadn't made people any less wary of her or her house. People did wonder what was going to happen to both of them. The church ladies heard she was sick and would be in the hospital indefinitely. Ruby heard Mr. Bell telling one of his employees that someone had better look after her house if she was gonna be gone for a long time. No one had come to check on it and her daddy worried that Mrs. Reed might not have any family to do so. Gramma was in favor of tearing it down completely.

"It's all covered up but you can tell that house is falling apart. She never had anyone over doing repairs. And all those vines and bushes?" She shook her head.

A couple of days after the playground conversation, Ruby went over to Mayson's house. She needed to check on the beehive there and after, once Mayson's dad went down to the basement to work, they pulled up the Discord server where Mayson had posted about the bug so they could read the responses.

"They're all interested but no one else has seen anything like what you saw. They agree it has to be an escaped experiment, though."

The channels were full of talk about all kinds of weird stuff: aliens, government cover-ups, planetary alignments, a whole discussion on how to be prepared when the Earth's magnetic poles reversed.

"Why is there a channel called 'Fluoride'?" Ruby asked.

"They think we're being poisoned by it being in the water."

"What?"

Mayson shook her head. "It's stupid, my dad says so."

"Does your mom know you posted about the bug here?"

"No, she doesn't come in this server, anymore." She got up to close the door, then spoke in a low voice. "She and my dad had a big fight about it a few months ago. He said she was spending too much time in these groups and getting all worked up and she said she needed to feel informed and he said that what she needed was community, real community, and she said people in the neighborhood treated her different because she's white."

"Wow. That's a lot. They said all that in front of you?"

"I was in the kitchen. They didn't know." She pulled her knees up and rested her chin on them, her face full of sadness. Ruby hadn't realized all that about Miz Trish. And she was just starting to understand better how the way everyone talked about her must really hurt Mayson. "My dad wanted her to take a break from here for a while and get more IRL friends. I think she only agreed because there was a whole drama with some really nasty trolls and the mods wouldn't do anything about them. I haven't seen them in the past couple days, so maybe they finally got kicked."

"Trolls suck."

They looked through the channels for a little while longer, not finding anything even close to what had been going on in their neighborhood.

"That thing probably did leave, like Alberto said, and ran back to where it came from," Mayson offered.

"Yeah. I hope so." Ruby didn't say the other thing she was thinking: Some part of her wished she'd found out what the bug was. That it was gone was less scary, but also less satisfying and way less interesting.

The Bug Club hadn't been any help. No one could identify it from her drawing and some people even said she must have imagined it. That part hurt. Ruby was a serious scientist—or she would be someday. She would never make things up about insects. It confirmed she was right not to tell any other adults about it, though.

When Ruby got home, her parents were sitting together in the TV room and she could tell from their faces they weren't happy about something. At first, she wondered if it was another theft, then her daddy called her in.

"We need to talk, young lady." It was almost never good when she got called "young lady." "I got an email from Mrs. Bailey today. She says that you've been disrespectful and defiant in class."

Ruby's jaw dropped. *What did she do that for?* "I apologized!" This did not make their frowns go away.

It wasn't fair. She had done what Miss Valya had suggested and told Mrs. Bailey that she was sorry for her tone and that she was wrong. Mrs. Bailey had said she accepted the apology. What was the problem?

"Why were you disrespectful in the first place?" Mama said.

"I was tired because I didn't get any sleep when they took Wit—I mean Mrs. Reed away, so I wasn't really thinking right. Miss Valya said that can happen when you're exhausted."

"Miss Valya?" Mama asked.

"School counselor," said Daddy.

"I talked to her when I got sent to the principal's office. She said I should apologize and so I did."

"Mrs. Bailey also said that you're being defiant in class and won't do the assignments she gives you," Daddy said.

"That's not true!"

"Ruby . . ." Mama said in her I'm-warning-you voice.

"It's not! I do all my assignments."

"Is that the whole truth? Because your track record hasn't been the best lately."

"You can look in my homework folder. I did every single one, even the boring ones." Ruby used to skip those assignments in elementary school until Mama and Daddy gave her a talking-to and said she couldn't do that simply because she already knew the answers. They clearly remembered this because they gave each other "a Look." What if they didn't believe her? She could feel even more punishment coming on and she did not want that. "I promise!"

"Okay, baby," Daddy said. "I'm going to come to your school tomorrow and talk to Mrs. Bailey and Principal Martinez and get all the details."

Now her daddy was going to see the principal? *Great,* she thought, *I really will be branded a bad kid.* Ruby went up to her room and tried not to cry. She couldn't believe that studying bugs for science—her favorite thing in the whole world—could cause her so much trouble. But it was true. That stupid giant bug had ruined everything.

CHAPTER FIFTEEN

The whole next day at school, Ruby's stomach twisted and turned with anxiety over what was going to happen at Daddy's meeting with the principal. He said he was going to work things out. But she was sure by the end of it, she would be in even more trouble. She was supposed to get the xCUBE back that night. Would they take it away for another two weeks? If so, she would die of boredom, she was certain.

In science class she didn't say one word to Mrs. Bailey. Not even when she knew the answers to questions. Better to not say anything if she couldn't say it respectfully.

Late in the day she was called to the office and all the tight knots in her tummy got tighter. Once she got there Mr. Segal smiled at her and told her to go on into the principal's office. Her daddy was in there sitting across from Mrs. Martinez. She was a very short Cuban woman with a crown of braids wrapped and piled on her head, which Ruby envied. Gramma used to braid her hair but got frustrated when Ruby wouldn't stop squirming or asking if it was done yet. Now the most she would do is put it in twists on special occasions.

"Hello Ruby, come sit down," the principal said. Her smile almost put Ruby at ease, then Mrs. Bailey came in and sat down as well. "Good, everyone is here. It seems we have some potential miscommunication and our goal here today is to clear that up. Okay?" she said, looking at Ruby.

"Okay, ma'am."

"Mrs. Bailey, in the email you sent Mr. Finley you said that Ruby has been defiant and won't do her assignments."

"I looked at her science folder last night and she's turned in every homework and worksheet, according to you," Daddy said. "What assignment is she not doing?"

"Pardon me, I should have been clearer," Mrs. Bailey said. "She won't pick an appropriate science fair project, despite my giving her a list to choose from."

"I thought you turned in your proposal already?" Daddy said to Ruby.

"I did. She doesn't like it," Ruby said. "She wanted me to pick one from her list."

"Because the project you proposed is far too advanced for you and you won't be able to do it well, which will result in a poor showing on Science Day." Mrs. Bailey turned to the principal. "If we have too many low scores it won't reflect well on the school."

She talked like Mrs. Martinez was going to be on her side. But the principal looked confused. Then Ruby saw her daddy sit up straighter and his face changed.

"How did you determine that the project was too advanced?" Mrs. Martinez asked.

"Well, I . . . I read the proposal."

She waited a second for Mrs. Bailey to say something else. When she didn't: "Did you give Ruby a chance to show she would be able to do the work?"

"I didn't think it was necessary—"

"Ruby," Mrs. Martinez said, cutting the teacher off, "what is your science fair project about?"

"It's about bees! They have a really, really good sense of smell and can find stuff up to two miles away. And you can train them to identify specific scents, just like dogs, but better than dogs!" She was nearly bouncing in her seat. "So I trained a hive of bees in my neighborhood to come to a specific feeder in the first phase, and then I trained them to associate two chemicals with the feeder, and next I'm going to show how they can identify the chemicals even when there's no sugar, then show how far they will follow the smell of the chemical. At the same time there's another hive in my neighborhood I'm using as a control. I didn't train those bees, so we'll see if they go to the chemical at all."

"And you've already completed part of the experiment?" Mrs. Martinez sounded impressed.

"Yes. I had to start in the summer because the bees act more erratic as it gets closer to winter. It's best to train them in summer when they aren't concerned about having enough food to store."

"This all sounds like something you had an adult do for you," Mrs. Bailey said. "That's against the rules."

"Excuse you?" Ruby's daddy, who had been smiling at her proudly, now turned to the teacher, not smiling. "My daughter is a gifted student who has always excelled above her grade level in science, which I know for a fact her elementary school teacher told you because I saw the letter. The only reason we didn't send her to Seven Hills Science is she begged us to go to the same school as all her friends. My wife and I were told she would get a high-quality science education here. Is that not the case?"

"Mr. Finley, there's no need to shout and get angry."

Ruby blinked, confused. Her daddy wasn't shouting and yeah, he wasn't happy, but he hadn't been angry. She wondered why Mrs. Bailey would say that.

"He has a point, Robin," Mrs. Martinez said. "Just now Ruby explained her project in a way that shows she understands it and has done the work."

"My daughter has been planning this experiment since May," Daddy said, his eyes locked on Mrs. Bailey. "She wrote out all the skills she learned specifically for this project in her proposal as well as where she learned them."

"I'm sure you had help learning how to handle the bees?" the principal asked.

"Yes ma'am. The people at Urban Beekeepers taught me what to do, and one of my neighbors who belongs to the group watches me to make sure I don't get hurt. But I do all the work."

"All of which sounds like it's within the bounds of acceptable help." She turned to the teacher. "Again, what is the problem?"

Mrs. Bailey opened her mouth a few times, then threw up her hands. "I guess there isn't one."

"So when you said that my daughter was 'defiant,' what you meant was she didn't want to scrap the project she's been working on for months to do one of your suggestions?" Daddy was angry now, Ruby could tell by the tightness in his jaw.

"She was extremely rude to me!"

"My understanding is she apologized for that. The day *before* you sent that email," Daddy said. "Now I do recognize that disrespect is not called for and we've had a discussion about that. However, it seems to me your real problem is this science fair thing."

"I agree," Mrs. Martinez said. "And I think Mrs. Bailey and I should have a conversation about that, don't you agree, Robin?"

The teacher pursed her lips and gave a short nod.

"Ruby, your project sounds fascinating and I can't wait to see your presentation on Science Day." That made her smile. Plus, the principal wasn't going to think she was a bad kid after all. "Mr. Finley, I will follow up with you on Monday. Thank you for coming in."

"Thank you," Daddy said, giving her a fist bump, then he reached out for Ruby's hand. "I'm going to take my daughter home early today, if that's all right?"

"I think under the circumstances, it is."

Mrs. Bailey made a little grunt, but no one seemed to care. Ruby and Daddy left the office and headed out to the car. He didn't speak the whole way there. And once they got in, he didn't turn the car on, just sat behind the wheel for a minute, quiet. Then he leaned over to kiss her forehead.

"Has Mrs. Bailey been saying things like that to you all the time? About you not being able to do advanced work?"

Ruby thought back. "I guess a couple times. Mostly about my project, though."

"How come you didn't tell me or your mama?"

"I talked to Mr. Lewis and he said he would help and so I didn't think it mattered."

Daddy chuckled. "You felt like you handled it, huh?"

"Yeah."

"I know I tell you this all the time, and I'm never gonna stop. I'm very proud of you. I admire how you always work to find solutions to problems or obstacles you encounter. That's what makes you a good scientist." Ruby beamed at him. Best compliment ever. "You don't have to handle *everything* by yourself, though. Me and your mama can help you, too."

She wondered if that included help with giant red bugs that ate elderly neighbors.

"So from now on whenever you have a problem with a teacher, even a small one, talk to us about it," Daddy said. "We can help you come up with a solution or step in if you need us to. That way we won't get to a point where you get so stressed out you say something you'll regret."

"Okay, I promise I'll do that."

"Thank you." He kissed her one more time before turning on the car. "I was gonna go visit Mrs. Reed in the hospital today. Do you wanna come or do you want me to drop you off at home first?"

"I wanna come with you."

"A'ight, let's go."

CHAPTER SIXTEEN

As they drove to the hospital, Daddy tried to prepare her. "Mrs. Reed's still in a coma. You know what that is?"

"When you're asleep but can't wake up?" Ruby said.

"Yeah, like that. A very deep sleep. She's hooked up to machines that make sure she breathes and gets nutrition. It'll look kinda like it did when your grandpa was in the hospital."

That wasn't a very happy memory. "Is Mrs. Reed gonna pass away like he did?"

"I don't know. That's one reason I'm going over there today, to get an update on her." Daddy squeezed her hand, and it looked like he needed a hug. She'd give him one before they went in.

At Christ Hospital it smelled the same way it had

when they had come there three years ago—rubbing alcohol mixed with medicine mixed with lemon. They walked down several long hallways until they got to an area called the ICU. Daddy went up to a dark-skinned Black man sitting on a bench outside one of the rooms.

"Hey Les," he said as they bumped elbows. "This is my little girl, Ruby."

"I'm pleased to meet you, Ruby. I'm Mr. Gaines," he said, and bumped her elbow, too. "Your dad talks about you all the time. He's very proud of you."

She smiled wide, and Daddy laughed. "We were just talking about that, huh?"

"Yep."

"How is she doing?" Daddy nodded toward the room and Ruby finally saw that Mrs. Reed was there in a bed. Like he'd warned her, she was hooked up to machines with tubes and wires all over. She seemed lonely.

"No change so far. The doctors are trying to determine where the cancer has metastasized."

Ruby stared at the old woman through the window in the hospital room door, only half listening to their conversation. The words *cancer* and *metastasized* she recognized too well. It was what they had said about Grandpa before he died. She wondered if somehow the red bug had given Mrs. Reed cancer, then she realized that didn't make sense. It did explain why the bug didn't eat her, maybe. Some insects and animals could smell infections, cancers, and other diseases. Bees could even detect Alzheimer's years before people got symptoms.

Looking at Mrs. Reed now—small for the big bed, ashy-skinned, frail—she didn't seem so scary or like a witch. Why had Ruby ever thought that?

Probably because that's what all the other kids said and the adults never corrected them. She didn't remember a time when Mrs. Reed's house wasn't all covered in vines and stuff and the dogs didn't chase people. No one had ever before told her or any kid she knew what Witchypoo's real name was. Everyone just called her Witchypoo. All the stories Ruby knew about her—how she would jump out at you from the bushes or how she purposely set her dogs on people or how she had a pentagram in her basement—all came from older kids. Now she wondered about what kind of person Mrs. Reed really was.

"Are you her son?" Ruby asked, walking over to Mr. Gaines.

"No, I'm her lawyer. She never had any children."

"You take care of her, though?"

Les looked sad for a second. "Not exactly. My grandfather was her lawyer when he was alive. Her and her husband." He looked over toward the room. "When he passed on I inherited her as a client and made sure the money her husband left paid the bills and such. I did it all over the phone. She didn't like coming out of the house and never wanted me to come in. My mother knew her a little and said she fell apart when her husband died."

Daddy nodded. "My wife's mama said the same. He was more outgoing than she was. After he was gone, she cut herself off from everyone."

Ruby went back to the little window while they kept talking about organizing a group of people to keep tabs on the house. She half listened in case they mentioned anything she didn't know already that might relate to the bug. Nothing specific, just arranging for someone to fix the exposed wiring and people to make sure the pipes didn't burst if Mrs. Reed was still in the hospital come winter. Ruby tuned them out and focused on the fragile-looking woman in the bed.

"I'm sorry I thought so many bad things about you," she whispered. "I'm glad we helped you before the bug killed you. I hope you get better."

* * *

Back in the car she and Daddy were quiet for a long time. Halfway home he swung into a DQ drive-thru and got her an ice cream. Strawberry, her favorite. Once she'd licked it down to the cone he looked over and laughed.

"Feel better?"

"Yeah." After a few more licks she remembered a question she'd wanted to ask. "What did Mr. Gaines mean when he said Mrs. Reed 'fell apart' after her husband died?"

Daddy made a deep sigh before he answered. "Remember the sadness you felt after your grandpa passed?"

Ruby didn't like to talk about it. Thinking of Grandpa still hurt; she missed him all the time.

"Everyone felt that way. Me, your mom . . . for Gramma, it was extra painful. They were together and loved each other a long, long time." He wiped a tear away. "Sometimes sadness and grief can overpower a person. They don't want to do anything they normally do because of the pain. That's what he meant. I think Mrs. Reed became very depressed when her husband died and, because she didn't have people looking out for her, her depression went untreated."

"She didn't want people to look out for her," Ruby said.

"True. That happens with people with mental health issues sometimes. Folks on the block respected her privacy—which is good. At the same time, it meant she didn't get the help she needed. They likely didn't realize she needed it. Back in the day people weren't as aware of mental health. It's still a problem in the Black community."

"Will she get better?"

"I don't know, baby. I hope so." They pulled up into the driveway and he handed her a napkin so she could wipe her face. "Don't tell Gramma I let you have ice cream before dinner."

She giggled. "I won't."

He pulled her into a side hug and kissed the top of her head and told her he loved her. Even if it was sad, she was glad they had done this trip together.

Before they went into the house, Ruby looked over at Mrs. Reed's. She hoped that bug had been caught by the government men and that they were locking it up forever for messin' with a sick old lady just because she had no one to look out for her.

CHAPTER SEVENTEEN

That night it had been officially two weeks since her punishment and Ruby was allowed to have her xCUBE back. To celebrate, Mama played *Super Sonic Smash* with her for a few hours after dinner. They had so much fun and made so much noise Gramma yelled at them both to quiet down, which made them giggle even louder.

The next morning Ruby decided she was going to spend her whole Saturday playing games and forgetting about the last couple of weeks. Just as she was about to get started, the doorbell rang and her mama called upstairs that Brandon was there to see her. He'd been so salty this past week, not talking to her at school and sharing his fancy food with everyone else. Ruby didn't feel like talking to him, especially now.

"Go away," she said when she came down to the screen door. "I'm busy."

"Ruby, wait!" he said before she could close the door. "I'm sorry, okay? Really, really sorry."

Brandon never apologized. She stopped and looked at him proper for the first time. He was . . . scared.

"Please come out and play," he pleaded. *Come out and play?* He never said stuff like that.

"What's wrong with you?"

"I just want you to come hang with us at the playground. Like normal." His tone was not normal. Something was wrong and he didn't want to say what where the adults could hear.

"A'ight. I'll get my bike . . ."

After letting Daddy know where she was going, she followed Brandon over to the playground. He was pedaling fast, like he was in a hurry, and she was about to yell after him to slow down when she came around the side of the old school and stopped dead in the street.

The playground was gone.

Gone, like, overnight gone. They rode by it on the bus every day and it had been there yesterday. Now the monkey bars and the slide and the swings and the carousel had disappeared.

Her brain felt like it wasn't working right but it

at least got her to pedal all the way over to Brandon, who was stopped by where the swings used to be. All that was left of them were the plastic seats. Now that she was up close, she saw other bits of plastic and wood from the equipment lying around on the pavement. Only the metal was gone.

That meant one thing.

"The bug," she whispered.

"When I saw this I knew you were right," Brandon said, his voice also soft. "There's no way someone came and tore this all down so quick. I'm sorry I didn't believe y'all."

"What are we gonna do?"

"We should get Jackie, she'll know."

"Let's get everyone," Ruby said. "You get her and Mayson, I'll get Hollie and Alberto."

They took off on their bikes again. Ruby's stomach was tight and she had to swallow hard to keep herself from throwing up. The bug hadn't left town. How big was it now? Would it start eating the whole neighborhood?

"Stop it," she said to herself. "We're going to get the others. We'll figure out what to do together." That was part of being a scientist, too. Collaborating to solve problems.

She raced over to Hollie's. Hollie was playing a game with Alberto over chat and, after Ruby whispered what happened in her ear, she told him to meet them at the playground ASAP.

Alberto arrived just before them and was already in full-blown freak-out mode, pacing in a circle and cursing in Spanish. *Asparagus* and *toothbrush* no longer cut it. Jackie was trying to hold it together, but she looked like she was about to cry as well.

"This is bad," Mayson said when she saw Ruby and Hollie. "So bad. We have to tell our parents!"

"They ain't gonna believe us!" Brandon said. "*Your* mom would, maybe, but people won't believe *her*."

"You shut up about my mom!"

"I didn't mean that in a mean way. I'm serious, Mayson!" he said when she shoved him hard. "Lots of adults think she's nuts. Clearly they wrong."

"We have proof now! If we show them this they can't say we're lying," Hollie said.

"They won't believe that an escaped experimental giant bug did it, though," Jackie said.

"Maybe not, but they can't ignore how weird this is. They have to investigate."

While they argued, Ruby studied the metal that was

still embedded in the ground. The way it was cut looked a lot like the edges of the iron fence at the church—melted. Definitely the bug. Then she saw drag marks like she'd seen in the ground at the church. They led off toward the school. The heavy padlock and chain that had been on the double doors was now gone.

"That must be where the bug is hiding," Ruby said, gesturing to the tracks that led to the school.

All the others jumped away from the building.

"Oh crap. It's inside?" Brandon sounded more scared than ever.

"If it is, then we can tell a grown-up and get them to go look for it," Hollie said.

"Girl, you know that's not gonna work," Jackie retorted. "Yeah, it's weird, but what, exactly, are we supposed to tell them?"

Ruby was torn. She wanted to do what Hollie and Mayson suggested. Her daddy had said she could come to him and Mama with her problems, that she didn't have to face them alone. They'd want to know something like this. But she knew that Jackie was also right. What could they tell the adults that would make them believe the story?

"We gotta at least try!" Brandon said. "There has to

be something we can say that will get them to go in and look. Maybe not 'It's a giant bug!' but, like, 'We think we know where the thieves are.'"

"Yeah, and what happens when they go in looking for thieves and find a huge government experiment that eats metal?" Mayson said. "If they don't know what they're getting into then they're gonna get hurt."

That sold Ruby. Whoever went to deal with the bug needed all the information. "We gotta get better evidence." Ruby looked around at all of them. "It's like the mystery shows. Science is the same. If you want people to believe you, you have to show them solid evidence that you're telling the truth."

"What are we supposed to do, take a picture of it?" Alberto tossed the suggestion off like a joke, but Jackie nodded.

"That's exactly what we have to do."

Hollie's and Brandon's objections and accusations of *Have you lost your mind?* overlapped. "She's right, though!" Ruby yelled over them. "We need pictures *and* videos. They can't ignore that."

"What if it covers its tracks again? That thing knows how to hide," Brandon pointed out.

"The last time, the bug knew people would be coming. This time it'll be a surprise. We sneak up on it, get proof, and escape," Ruby said. "Even if it hides again, we can still show the pictures to our parents or Mr. Harshaw or anyone else until someone believes us."

"And if no one does?" Alberto asked.

"We put it on the internet," Mayson answered. "That's how those men from the government knew where to find it before, right? We can tweet about it."

Mayson and Jackie were united; Hollie and Brandon didn't look sure.

Alberto started pacing back and forth again. "One thing none of y'all are thinking about: What if it attacks *us*? How are we gonna fight a giant bug?"

"We don't fight it," Jackie said. "We only need a way to keep it from coming after us."

They all looked at each other waiting for someone to come up with a good answer. "I got it!" Ruby clapped her hands. "Gramma's homemade bug-killing juice."

"Which works on normal bugs," Hollie said.

"It's strong, though. If it doesn't actually kill the thing, a face full of that stuff will definitely slow it down." Ruby could see her cousin still needed convincing. "We need something better than a spray bottle though, so we don't have to get too close."

And then the answer came to her in a burst of inspiration. "Like a water gun!"

"Absolute genius," Alberto said, and stood still, finally.

"We have one of those that can spray, like, fifty feet," Mayson said.

"Yeah, same," Alberto agreed. "Might have two or three."

"We have about twenty-five million at my house," Brandon said.

"That mean you're in?" Ruby asked. Brandon looked over at Hollie, unsure.

"I still say we should try to tell an adult." Hollie nodded at the school doors. "Because I do not want to go in there."

"How about this," Jackie said. "You and Brandon go find Mr. Harshaw and try to convince him. Mayson, you and Alberto get all the water guns you can find. Ruby, you go make a bunch of bug-killing juice to fill them."

"We need cameras, too. My dad has a couple small digital cameras he never uses. I can find them," Mayson offered.

"I'll bring my smartphone," Jackie said.

"*If* it comes to that, I can get Frankie Lee's smartphone," Hollie said. "He's on punishment and I know where my mama keeps it."

Brandon snapped his fingers. "I'll get some walkies

from our house, too. My brothers always get them for Christmas but never use them. That way we'll have a way to communicate instantly if we get separated."

"Good idea." Jackie gave him a playful knock on the head. "Let's meet at Ruby's house in an hour with everything, okay?"

They all agreed, then hopped on their bikes to their different destinations. This time Ruby felt much more hopeful. They were going to get the proof, save their neighborhood, and avenge Witchypoo.

Ruby knew where Gramma kept all her supplies for making homemade concoctions. Bug juice was just one; she also mixed her own cleaning supplies and natural insecticides for the garden. That meant she bought in bulk, and Ruby was able to find giant bottles of vinegar and rubbing alcohol in the basement. Gramma added peppermint and cinnamon oils to her bug recipe, so Ruby dumped them in, too. She also grabbed a bottle of ghost pepper sauce from the kitchen when Daddy wasn't looking and poured a bunch of it in the mix. It smelled gross and made her eyes water, which she took as a good sign. By the time the others came down, the whole back room of the basement reeked of it.

Ruby opened the basement door to the backyard to air the room out just as Hollie and Brandon showed up with more water guns. "I guess Mr. Harshaw didn't believe you?"

"No, thanks to Brandon," Hollie said.

"Not you saying that was *my* fault!"

"I tried to tell Mr. Harshaw I was worried there was someone or something dangerous in the old school—"

Brandon interrupted. "You didn't say 'dangerous,' you said 'concerning,' like that was going to make him do something."

"And genius here started talking about how it ate metal and gave Witchypoo cancer." Hollie rolled her eyes. "Mr. Harshaw told him to stop spreading misinformation about Mrs. Reed—"

"Which I wasn't!"

"—and that if someone was in the school, they might be seeking shelter and he didn't want to involve the police until the CCP can assess the situation."

"In five to ten business days." Brandon's sarcastic tone got him flicked in the head, courtesy of Hollie.

"So now I guess we'll have to go with your plan." She held up her brother's smartphone. "If Frankie Lee finds out I have this he will kill me."

"If we expose the bug, he won't even care," Ruby

said, while Jackie and Alberto started carefully pouring the bug-killing juice into the water guns.

Jackie divided the supplies among them—everyone got a walkie-talkie and a water gun; Hollie, Jackie, Mayson, and Brandon got the cameras and phones—then gave them their instructions.

"We split up into two groups. Me and Hollie will lead."

"Why do y'all get to lead?" Brandon said.

"Because we're the oldest and because I say so."

Brandon huffed, but Hollie pointed one of the water guns at him. "Hush."

Jackie continued. "Each group takes one floor. You see anything, you tell the other group over the walkies. You see that bug? You get a picture or video and you RUN. Got it?"

"Got it," they all echoed.

They left out the basement door so they wouldn't encounter Ruby's daddy or gramma but just then her mama pulled up into the driveway. "Y'all going out to play? You look like you're about to invade a small country."

"We're making a movie, Miz Anna," Brandon said.

"Have fun then!"

Ruby went over and hugged her hard. "Love you, Mama."

"Love you back, baby."

If Mama was suspicious of what they were doing, she didn't show it. Ruby made sure to smile and wave like she always did before she followed the others on her bike. They would find the bug, get the proof, and then tell her parents about it. Daddy had said she was a good scientist and could count on him and Mama to help, so she had to believe they would fix things once they were sure it was the truth. All she had to do was take one good picture and everything would be okay.

All right, big red bug: here we come.

CHAPTER EIGHTEEN

When they got back to the school they saw a group of adults gathered near the playground. They must have thought the sudden disappearance of the equipment was suspicious, too. Ruby spotted Miz Connor, one of the church ladies, taking pictures.

"How are we supposed to get in with all of them around?" Hollie asked.

Jackie turned her bike and started toward the other end of the building. "There's a busted door down on the other side, too."

Hollie looked scandalized as she followed.

Once they got down there and locked their bikes, Jackie decided who was on which team while Ruby gave everyone their water guns. Brandon and Mayson with her, Ruby and Alberto with Hollie.

"Do *not* go off alone," Jackie commanded. "We stay safe if we stay together."

They all promised, then headed in, Hollie and her team taking the first floor and Jackie's the second.

For the first five minutes Ruby could barely hear anything over her heart thundering in her ears. She was excited and scared and breathing too fast. She expected the bug to come up on them any second now, and her whole body shook, ready for it.

That didn't happen. With Hollie in the lead they walked quietly down the hall, the only light coming in from the classrooms on their left.

"Our last homeroom," Alberto said, after peeking in to make sure the bug wasn't there. "It looks so sad without our art on the wall."

Ruby agreed. All the rooms gave her a creepy vibe, the way they looked abandoned or ransacked. The science classroom especially so, since all the special equipment was gone. There was nothing left in any of the classrooms but old desks and chairs, dust, and spiderwebs. Normal ones.

"Remember how gross the bathrooms were?" Hollie whispered.

"However gross the girls' ones were," Alberto said in a low voice, "it can't have been as bad as the boys'."

"Yeah but boy's bathrooms are always gross," Ruby said, which earned her a raspberry.

They got almost to the end of the hall when Hollie poked her head in a classroom, then walked on. "Nothing."

Ruby glanced in and realized she meant literally nothing. No desks, no chairs. "Wait!" she whisper-shouted.

"What?"

"No furniture. The desks we saw in the other rooms were mostly metal, right?"

A light went on behind Hollie's eyes. "Oh . . ."

"We're getting close, aren't we?" Alberto whispered, not looking too pleased.

"I think so. Let's keep going this way." Hollie raised the water gun like she was going to shoot, the way they'd seen cops do on TV. Ruby did the same while Alberto got the camera ready.

The next few classrooms were just like that one. No furniture. Also no sign of anything else. When they came to the other end of the school, the three of them had to crouch down and crab walk past the windows so the adults on the other side wouldn't see them. Ruby caught some of their conversation—they were wondering if the city had torn down the playground. *If only*, she thought. Then she noticed the floor.

"Y'all, look!"

There were drag marks leading from the door and around the corner. Deep ones. They were on the right track. The marks kept on down the other hall and ended at a set of double doors.

"What's behind these?" Alberto asked. "I don't remember us being allowed in here."

"I don't know," Hollie said, her voice now even softer. "It's not a classroom. Probably a storage room?"

"Probably a lair now." Alberto was not being helpful.

"Okay, turn your camera on," Hollie said. "Ruby, you're gonna open the door."

"Why me?"

"Because I have the other camera and when you open it we gotta be ready to start taking pictures and run," Hollie said.

"Fine," she said, but made sure her water gun was ready, too.

One hand on that, the other hand on the knob, she counted down: "Three . . . two . . . one!" then yanked on the door.

Almost too late they realized there wasn't a room on

the other side, but a staircase. Hollie pulled back from falling down it just in time but overcompensated, landing on her bottom. "Ow!"

"I didn't know this place had a basement," Ruby said while helping her up.

"Every place has a basement." Alberto looked around the inside and outside of the door. "No light switch."

"It has to be down there."

"Close the door." Hollie pulled out her walkie-talkie. "Hey Jackie, we found a door to the basement and that thing is definitely down there."

"We're coming," Jackie answered once Hollie told her where they were.

Ruby's heart was back to beating very loud and very fast. She kept the water gun pointed at the door (just in case) and tried to be brave, hoping they would hear the bug if it started coming up the stairs. The last time she was close to it, it had been in her mason jar. Right now she couldn't remember if it had made a little clink-clink noise when it moved around. Was it still so quiet now that it was big? She hoped not.

It felt like forever before the others joined them and saw the drag marks.

"Yeah, it's down there," Jackie said. "Are there lights?"

Alberto shook his head. "Not that I can find. It looked pitch-black when we first opened the door. We'll need you two to use the flashlights on the phones to see."

"Nuh-uh." Brandon was walking backward away from the door. "I am not going down into some dark basement."

"Brandon—" Jackie reached out for him and he danced away.

"No! This is how Black people get killed in horror movies!"

"Shhh!" they all hissed at him.

"People die in horror movies 'cause they go off alone with no weapons," Hollie said. "We got weapons. We go as a group."

Brandon looked at each of them, hoping for someone else to agree with him. As scared as Ruby was, she was determined to get this thing. "We protect each other."

"Fine," Brandon growled. "If I die, I'm telling all y'all's ancestors on you."

Jackie and Hollie started recording video, which kept the flashlights on, and went down first. The staircase ended in a large space that looked very basementy, with pipes and ducts running along the ceiling and a concrete floor and exposed drywall. It smelled moldy, and a couple of them lifted their shirts over their noses to block it. As the lights swept around the room they landed on piles of junk—old textbooks, pink insulation, and other things that proved why students were never allowed down there. They didn't see anything out of the ordinary, and the floor was so dirty that it was hard to tell if there were more drag marks. Jackie whispered that they should spread out a little. No one wanted to get very far from her or Hollie, though.

Mayson crept over to a door, then made a small noise to get their attention. "I don't think it's locked."

Jackie came over to shine a light on it. "I'll open it and you look inside, okay?"

She nodded, then got her water gun ready. Jackie pulled the door open enough for her to peek in, which she did. And then Mayson screamed.

The sudden noise made Ruby's heart jump out of her and the fear behind it froze her in place. She was so freaked out she did not notice that the large pile of stuff up against the wall next to her was moving until something burst out of it in her direction.

All Ruby saw when she turned her head was red. Something red coming at her. Something big. Bigger than a dog. Bigger than a horse. Big, big, big and it was moving toward her and without thinking she started spraying the bug juice at it and screaming herself. There was another terrible noise. It came from the direction she'd been shooting, and that meant she'd hit it, right? So her feet decided it was time to run, and she grabbed for Hollie's hand—Hollie had been right there next to her just a second ago—but she touched something that was not a hand. It was too hard for a hand. And before her brain could begin to understand what she had felt, she was running in the direction of the staircase (she hoped) and away from that terrible noise.

A sharp pain in her leg made her scream—*It's got me, it's got me!*—and she tried to keep running. But she couldn't. Her legs slowed and her thoughts slowed and just before her vision went black she thought:

This must be what it's like for a fly.

CHAPTER NINETEEN

Ruby woke up to a sharp pain at the base of her neck. For a few seconds she couldn't see: her vision was fuzzy and the room was dark. She also couldn't remember where she was or how she got there. Her body felt weird. It took another few seconds for her to realize it felt weird because she was wrapped up like a mummy. Not lying down, though, upright. High upright. Her body was attached to the wall! No matter how hard she struggled, her arms and legs would not move.

Got to get out before—

Before—

Then she saw them. Bugs. Six of them. Just like the one she saw before, but bigger. Much bigger. Ruby had seen a rhino up close at the zoo last summer and the bugs' bodies looked around that size, not counting the very, very long legs that looked like they were ten feet long. Their green eyes were on her, glittering.

Ruby screamed.

//Stop.

She struggled harder and it made no difference.

//Please, stop.

Those things were going to eat her. She needed her mama and her daddy and her gramma . . . If they could just hear her screaming!

//You MUST STOP!

One of the bugs skittered over to her and Ruby knew she was about to die. It pointed a long leg at her and the webbing covering her body moved up until it covered her mouth, too, and muffled her screams.

//That noise is very annoying, please do not make it again.

Ruby was hearing a voice, she finally realized. It was sort of coming from inside her head and also sort of like an out-loud sound.

//If I uncover your mouth do you promise not to make that noise?

Was the bug talking to her? How? She peered at its face. It did have a mouth or ant-like mandibles that seemed like a mouth. But those weren't moving.

//Well?

It wanted her to stop screaming. If she didn't scream, how would anyone find her? Then again, she was in a basement in an abandoned school. Probably no one could hear her, anyway. She nodded yes, hoping the bug understood.

//Good.

It pointed a leg at her again and the webbing stuff moved back down to her shoulders.

//Now—

"Let me go! I want to go home! You can't keep me here! I'm not like Witchypoo, my parents will care I'm gone and they'll look for me and they'll call someone if you eat me and you can't eat me because I taste bad and everyone knows humans taste bad!"

//Are you done?

This was not the response she had expected.

//I am not going to eat you. Why do you think I want to eat you?

"You were gonna eat Witchypoo! Until I sent people to stop you."

//Do you mean the geriatric human female who lives near you? I most certainly was not going to eat her. How disgusting!

Ruby's fear was giving way to anger. A part of her

said she needed to stop talking and another part said the bug was going to kill her anyway, so she might as well tell it off. "Then why did you wrap her up in your webbing?"

//To save her life.

Another response she wasn't expecting. "What?"

//She had a disease of the cells, causing her significant internal harm. I wrapped her in a "webbing," as you call it, to put her in stasis so the disease could not progress. I tried to correct the problem. My understanding of your anatomy is limited. Also, *someone* alerted the authorities to my presence and I had to abandon her.

The bug had some nerve acting like Ruby was the bad guy in all this! Ruby was about to argue when something more important occurred to her.

"Wait a minute, how is it I can hear and understand you?"

//Finally, a useful question. I implanted nanotech into you that transmits my communication directly to your brain and translates it into a format you can understand.

"YOU IMPLANTED ME!?" The vision of parasitic wasps implanting their eggs inside other creatures raced through her mind again and she started screaming once more. Right away, the web she was wrapped in covered the lower part of her face again.

//No! No more of that noise, *please*!

Ruby glared at the bug so hard.

//The nanotech won't hurt you.

After a few seconds the web released her mouth. Ruby didn't scream.

"Did you implant Mrs. Reed, too? Are your babies going to burst out of her?"

//You have very strange ideas.

"You are a giant red bug! If you're possible, then anything is possible."

//Not *anything*. Many things you don't understand are possible. I am not a bug, as you call them. I'm not from this planet.

"You're . . . you're an alien?" This was too much. Ruby's vision started going black around the edges and she felt like she was going to slip away.

//From your perspective, I am an alien. I come from a planet outside of this solar system, as you call it.

"And you're here to invade us?" Her voice was small and scared because she felt small and scared. Scientists were still hypothesizing whether aliens existed. Most movies and TV shows she'd seen said that, if they did, they would probably attack Earth. Especially the ones that were giant and scary-looking. "Is that why there are so many of you?"

//There is only one of me.

The bug skittered over to the others and tapped each of them with a leg. None reacted.

//These are my discarded exoskeletons. I am using them to build a craft that will take me home. I was in the middle of work when you and the other small humans in your group interrupted me. I could not have you going to tell others. I am almost done with my craft and need more time to complete it.

It came back over to her.

//You are very rude small humans, you know! First you put me inside a container without asking, then you send a spy device to record me, and then you come to my workspace and make that horrible noise, and then you burn my eye with that liquid. So rude.

Ruby couldn't believe this was happening. It was the most ridiculous conversation in the whole history of everything.

"You're rude, too! You made those G-men come to our neighborhood. And then you stole all that metal. And you messed up Mrs. Reed's house. And, oh yeah, you ATE our PLAYGROUND!"

The bug, which had been standing very tall on its legs, dropped down and pulled them in closer to its body, almost like it was afraid.

//I apologize. I needed the metal. I had to eat and eat and eat to grow fast to make and discard enough exoskeleton to craft a vessel powerful enough to leave the planet. I'm so close. However, the metal in this building did not meet my needs so I had to eat what was right outside. I can't stay on this planet much longer without being detected.

Ruby's fear and anger melted away, immediately replaced by curiosity. "Wow, you can do that? Make a spaceship out of your own exoskeletons?"

The bug stood up at its full height again.

//Indeed. It's how my kind explore the space between planets.

"How do you make the circuits and conductors and stuff?"

//My webbing, as you call it. It has many properties, including the ability to route electricity.

"That's so cool. Beyond cool."

//I think that is a positive statement.

"It is." Ruby laughed. Then it hit her how very weird this all was. She was having a conversation with an alien bug like it was nothing. There were a million questions buzzing through her brain, but she decided to start at the beginning: "Why did you come here to Earth?"

//I am a scientist. I came to this planet to research you.

"I'm a scientist, too! That's why I put you in the mason jar. I wanted to study you."

//I would *not* have put you in a container. Not without consent.

"I'm sorry about that. I thought you were an Earth insect and we can't get, uh, consent from insects when we study them. It's not like we can communicate."

//Have you tried? I think humans think they are so far above the other life-forms on this planet that they don't have to listen and that other life-forms have nothing to say. I can tell you, having had discussions with many of them, they do.

Ruby had no idea what to say to that. This was a lot to take in all at once.

The bug started skittering around, moving pieces of metal off to another room Ruby couldn't see inside. Its voice was still clear.

//You are a very hasty species, I must say. I was just at the edge of your atmosphere when my vessel was incapacitated by an energy I didn't recognize.

No *Hello*, no *Please state your business*, just attacks! I never would have come if I knew I would receive such a welcome.

Now everything was making sense. This was why the government men had shown up. They must have been the ones that shot down the vessel.

//Then I had to make an emergency landing because my ship was damaged. I consumed it quickly, hoping to avoid detection. I thought the vegetation would be enough to conceal me. Until *you* captured me.

"I said sorry . . ."

//I created a ship in the geriatric female's dwelling that I thought would be powerful enough to take me home. It was not. And since other humans came there, I looked for a place without humans. The woman I tried to help was in no condition to harm me. Not like the ones who came looking. I was afraid they would.

"Did you call for help?" Ruby asked when the bug came back into the room. "Or are you too far away from your planet to contact your family?"

It tucked back in again, making itself seem small.

//No, I did not. I could have. I wanted to try and solve the problem alone because . . . I am not supposed to be here.

"On Earth?"

//Yes. I wanted to do revolutionary research so I can join a hive for exceptional scientists. My kind have not come here in many of your cycles. I didn't know your technology would be advanced enough to detect me. This planet is not well documented. I wanted to impress my progenitors by doing so.

"And they wouldn't let you?"

//I'm not supposed to leave my own solar system without supervision.

"Why?"

The bug pulled its legs in even more.

//I am not yet fully mature.

"You're just a kid? Like us?!" Ruby almost laughed, then stopped, thinking the bug might think she was laughing at it. "We're not supposed to leave the neighborhood alone, either."

//If I called for help, my siblings and progenitors would know I had broken the rules. Punishment would follow.

Parents were the same all across space.

"Do you think they're looking for you now? It's been a while."

//Perhaps. And they won't know that humans will

be able to detect them. This is why I must complete my vessel and go. I need just another part of this day. And I need your help.

"Me? I don't know nothing about spaceships."

//Not with the ship. I need you to convince the other small humans to leave this building and not tell the authorities I am here. They seem to trust you. They'll listen to what you say.

"They're all still here?" Ruby had been so terrified, and then so surprised, that she hadn't thought about what had happened to the others.

//In stasis, unconscious. They're quite safe.

Ruby had her fists all clenched up and now she could relax. Hollie and the others were okay, and not scared out of their minds like she had been. "I dunno if I can get them to stay quiet about this. No offense, but giant alien bugs freak us humans out. They'll probably be too scared."

//Please try. Once I complete my vessel I will leave and never cause you trouble again. If I'm detected, I'll have to fight and harm humans. That behavior is against our rules.

"I don't want you to have to fight, either. I'll do my best, promise."

The bug pointed a leg at her and the webbing slid down the wall and unraveled, leaving her safe on the ground.

//Thank you. The other four are in the room you first entered.

Ruby went to go that way, then stopped. "The other four?"

//Yes.

"Uh . . ."

//Yes?

"We got a problem."

//What?

"I came here with *five* other people."

CHAPTER TWENTY

Ruby ran into the other room and saw her friends covered up in the ropy, reddish webbing. Only their faces were showing and it took a second for Ruby to fight the panic at seeing them this way, eyes closed and looking mummified. They were attached to pipes along the wall so they stayed upright. When she got closer she could tell everyone was breathing. Hollie, Jackie, Mayson, Alberto . . . Brandon was the one missing. He must have run back up the stairs in all the commotion.

He left us behind, that brat! she thought, then stopped herself. Of course he ran. Not like they could have fought the bug if it had been out to kill them. He must have gone to get help. How long until someone came?

She went back into the other room. "Brandon is

probably getting his parents or the police right now. That means they're gonna come look for us."

The bug skittered back and forth, pacing like Alberto did when he was anxious.

//This is not good. I need more time. I cannot start over again!

Without a phone she had no idea how long she'd been down there or how soon Brandon would bring people back to rescue them. Could be just a few minutes. And if they came in nothing good would come from it. Ruby closed her eyes and tried to force her brain to come up with an idea to help.

"Wait, you tricked those government men the day I—the day you got here. They found something they thought was you. How did you do that?"

//I shed a layer of exoskeleton and sent it away from my hiding place with remote control. They must know it was a false me by now, I set it to self-destruct. If I do the same again, that will not deter them. They'll keep looking.

If they weren't so pressed for time Ruby would want every detail because that sounded amazing! She forced herself to focus. "This time, don't let them catch it. Make it run away, but slow enough they chase it, and keep doing that until you're done building your spaceship."

The bug stopped pacing.

//That is an excellent idea. However, you will have to control the exoskeleton.

"Me?"

//Yes. I won't be able to operate it and work on my vessel simultaneously. I can create an interface for you to do so.

A bunch of objections to this plan went through her head. What if she couldn't get the hang of the interface? Or broke the exoskeleton? She took a deep breath and pushed those thoughts away. If she could reach level forty in *Golden Scarab II,* she could do this.

The bug had gone back to the other room, so she followed it in. The other exoskeletons weren't complete, she could see that now. They were missing legs or parts of the thorax—*was that even the right word for an alien body?* she wondered—or heads. The bug went to the most complete one.

//I can make this one functional in moments.

It went deeper into the basement and Ruby again followed, stopping as she turned a corner to stare wide-eyed at what she saw there. Another bug! Even bigger and redder than the one skittering around it. This must be the ship it was building. It didn't look exactly like the bug—it had twelve legs instead of six, some sticking out from the sides and some on top of the body, and it was twice as wide.

"Whoa," was all she could say.

Walking closer—slowly—she could see how there were panels of the red exoskeleton layered on top of each other, a little like a reptile's scales. She wondered how many times it had had to shed to make this. And how would it get to space? The ship didn't look like it had rockets.

"How does it work? Our space shuttles need huge tanks of fuel to get to space. This doesn't have anything like that."

//Yes, your methods of escaping the planet's gravitational force are primitive, from what I've seen, the bug said as it carried a panel of exoskeleton back into the other room.

//You have not yet grasped how to manipulate gravity and energy the way my kind do.

"I, uh, I'm not sure what that means." Something she hated to admit, especially to a fellow scientist. Then again, how else did scientists learn but by asking questions?

//You know of gravity, yes? The gravitational field of any large body, such as a planet or a star, attracts smaller bodies to it. My kind also know how to do the reverse. To manipulate the gravitational field to push away from large bodies, or navigate around them.

Ruby thought of how spiders used electricity to fly and wondered if what the bug was talking about was something like that.

//Your planet resonates at a different frequency than my own, and I misjudged how powerful the ship had to be the first time. This one will push me free of the atmosphere.

"So. Cool."

//I have completed the exoskeleton. I need you for the interface.

After one last look at the spaceship, Ruby walked back to the other room and stood beside the bug. It had several long, narrow pieces of metal arranged in a hexagon. While she watched, it wove the web material around them, its legs moving so fast she couldn't keep up. Ruby had to close her eyes to stop herself from getting dizzy. In a minute the bug was done and laid the thing on the ground.

//Stand here, please.

Ruby stepped on the pad and it lit up immediately, surrounding her with blue and green lights. No, not just lights, she realized. Holograms!

"Whoa," she said again.

Two buttons floated up in front of her.

//Use the left one to go side to side, use the right one to go forward and back.

Reaching up, she put her fingers where she saw the buttons and they responded as if touched, though nothing was there. She slid one up and the empty exoskeleton moved forward a step. Going higher made it go much faster and she almost crashed it into the wall.

"Sorry! These controls are sensitive." While she got used to them, she nodded toward some discarded materials in a corner. "You should wrap those up in bundles so they look like bodies, then attach them to the robobug."

//Robobug? it said, moving to do as she suggested.

"Yeah. Robot bug. Robobug!"

//I am not a bug.

"Roboalien doesn't sound as good. What's your actual name, then?"

//You would not be able to understand it.

"Can I give you a code name? I can't keep calling you 'the bug' in my head. Or 'it.' Do your, uh, kind have genders? Pronouns?"

//The equivalent to your species is female. And yes, a code name is a good idea.

She thought on it for a second. "How about Rose, since you're red? I'm Ruby, so we can be Ruby and Rose."

Rose did something like a dance, legs moving back and forth in quick, short movements.

//I like this code name. Rose. And Ruby.

Rose worked on spinning her webbing around kid-shaped bundles while Ruby practiced moving the robobug around and avoiding the wall. Most of the time.

After a few minutes, she started to wonder why they hadn't heard anyone coming. It had to have been at least a half hour since they all came down here. Did Brandon not escape? Was he hurt somewhere upstairs? Ruby was about to go look when a rapid beeping came from the room with the spaceship.

//Someone has entered the building. You must lead them away.

Ruby didn't feel ready. She still didn't have very good control over the robobug. Didn't matter. They were out of time.

She took a deep breath. "Okay. Let's do this."

CHAPTER TWENTY-ONE

Once Ruby had guided the robobug out of the room, camera displays popped up in the holograms around her so she could control it remotely. She could see forward, on both sides, and behind the machine. That didn't make getting it up the stairs any easier since she was still clumsy with the controls. Once it got through the door and onto the first floor she heard voices saying "Something's coming!" Luckily, the robobug had audio to go along with the video. The cameras showed two cops standing by the doors to the outside and they both looked terrified.

"Sorry," Ruby said, then pushed the button to run the robobug right at them.

One officer turned and booked it out the door, but

the other shot at the robobug several times before following him. She didn't see any warning signs that the bullets had done damage and figured the exoskeleton was handling it. So she kept going and the robobug burst out of the double doors next to where the playground used to be, taking some of the frame with it. There were other people outside, all shouting after the cops.

And then they saw the giant red bug coming after them. Chaos erupted.

People ran in all directions, some grabbing up kids who'd also gathered in the crowd. She turned toward the police car parked on the street and saw Brandon standing with Mr. Harshaw next to it. She heard him say, "See, I told y'all!" before he noticed the robobug facing his way. Mr. Harshaw grabbed his arm and pulled him toward one of the houses. Ruby pushed the bug a few more steps away from the building, waiting for people to get far enough away so they weren't in danger of being stepped on. Someone off to the left said, "It has them kids!" *Good, the bundles worked,* Ruby thought. Now to lead the cops away.

She ran at the police car then made a hard turn to run up the street toward Reading Road, knowing exactly where she wanted to go. A golf course bordered the north end of the neighborhood and it was the perfect place to keep everyone occupied without doing damage to houses. A thing she tried not to do as she pushed down the block.

Reading Road was a wide, four-lane street, which meant less chance of knocking over a building but more chance of getting hit by cars, which happened several times as she plowed into traffic. One hybrid sideswiped the robobug's leg as it tried to get away and she almost stopped to stomp on it before checking her instinct.

This isn't a game, Ruby had to remind herself. *They're real people. Can't hurt them.*

Good thing the cars started getting out of the way as she skittered on. People were rushing to avoid the giant red thing in the road. All except the police, who were right behind her. She kept guiding the robobug forward, then crashed through a fence at the far end of the golf course. Maybe the police would take the regular entrance, maybe not. All she had to do was keep them engaged.

When she finally saw cars behind her again, it wasn't just black-and-white cop cars, but regular ones, too. All of them driving across the green grass in her direction. This had not been in the plan. *Who were those people?* she wondered. Then she recognized a truck—it belonged to Jackie's parents. Ruby's neighbors were chasing her, too!

"Stick to the plan," she said to herself, then ran the robobug deeper into the golf course. The legs were tearing up the neatly trimmed grass, pulling up huge chunks of dirt and leaving holes as she went. It would make her easy to track, so all the better.

For over fifteen minutes Ruby played cat and mouse with the cars following her, darting back and forth, sometimes rushing right at them, sometimes away, doing her best not to hurt anyone. Especially when she saw that all the non–cop cars had people she knew in them, including her daddy. When she recognized him, her heart beat hard knowing he must think she was in danger and was out there risking his life to save her.

"I'm okay, Daddy." When this was over she would have to find some way to say she was sorry.

Ruby was so focused on moving the robobug around that she didn't see that five other cop cars had zoomed into the area until they surrounded her. Each way she turned there was a car and not enough space between them to run through safely. She stopped moving the robobug and tried to decide what to do next. Should she step on one car and hope the cops were smart enough to get out in time? Then she saw that a few of them had gotten out already and were pointing very big guns in her direction.

"No!" someone yelled. "You'll hit the kids!"

"Stand down!" Mr. Harshaw yelled at the cops.

"How else do you expect us to stop it!" one of them yelled back.

Just then Rose skittered by Ruby in the basement at top speed.

"You're done already?" Ruby asked.

//Not yet. However, I have an idea.

Have to keep this up, then, Ruby thought. "Can the robobug do that gravitational-field-manipulation thing?"

A big green button popped up right in front of her face.

"Yesssss!" She pushed it, and the robobug leaped into the sky and landed just beyond the circle of cars.

There were some shouts and curses behind her that, at first, she didn't pay attention to. But checking the rear camera view, she saw several people running toward one of the wrapped-up bundles lying on the grass.

"Uh-oh, must have fallen off."

Turning was not as easy as moving forward, and by the time she was back around in that direction Jackie's mom, Miz Pam, was pulling the webbing off the bundle. Once she saw there was nothing but junk inside she wailed, from relief or grief Ruby couldn't tell. Her stomach clenched in sympathy but she had to push it down. Because now they knew she and the other kids weren't in those bundles.

"Our cover's blown!" she shouted in the direction Rose went.

//I don't know what that means.

"They know me and the others aren't out there with the robobug."

Rose skittered by again.

//No matter. I implemented my idea. Move the robobug to an area that is very open.

"Got it." Ruby had been keeping the legs in motion the whole time to stay ahead of the cops and everyone else who now had no reason to hold their fire. Pushing the forward control up as high as it went, she raced it out to the middle of the golf course. "Now what?"

//Hold the gravitational control button for a count of five, then let go.

The green button popped up again and Ruby did as she was told, counting and trying not to get dizzy as the cameras showed the robobug going up, up, up . . . "Five!" She let go, and the bug hovered for a millisecond before tumbling down, down, down.

"Get back. BACK!" people on the ground yelled.

There was a loud crash and then the cameras cut out. The golf course probably had a huge hole in the center now but Ruby couldn't know for sure. The exoskeleton had broken apart on impact.

"Bye, robobug," Ruby said, and sighed.

//Excellent. Now, you must get your friends out of the building as fast as you can. I will ensure no one comes back in.

"Okay," Ruby said, and ran back into the other room. Then she stopped. "I wish you could stay longer. I wanna know all about how your spaceship works and the planet you come from and a billion other things."

//Perhaps I will be able to return in the future. If I do, I will find you and tell you everything.

"That would be amazeballs. Good luck getting home and avoiding punishment."

//Thank you, Ruby.

She waved, then went to the other room. Her friends were now lying on the floor. After a few seconds, Ruby chose to wake Jackie up first. She'd help her get everyone out.

"Come on, come on," she said while shaking Jackie, pretending to be scared. The older girl opened her eyes and sat up fast.

"What—where—"

"We're in the basement. The bug thing captured us. It went off somewhere and I got free. I don't know when it's coming back, so we gotta go!" Ruby tried to put as much urgency and fear in her voice as she could, hoping Jackie would accept the story and run.

"Where're the others?" Jackie said, pulling the rest of the webbing off her.

"Right here."

They worked together to shake Hollie, Alberto, and Mayson awake, get them free, and repeat the story. The web material came off easily—too easily. Ruby hoped they were all too freaked out to notice. "Let's go!"

"Wait, where's Brandon?" Hollie asked, frantically looking around.

Shoot, she thought. She hadn't counted on them asking. Thinking fast as she grabbed hands and pulled toward the door, she said: "Not down here. I looked all around before I found y'all. He must have run."

"What if he's hidden somewhere, though?" Hollie wasn't budging.

"Then we get an adult to come for him," Jackie said, and grabbed her other arm. "If we stay here and that thing comes back we all gonna die!"

Finally, Hollie let them drag her along and up the stairs, where they saw the damage the robobug had done to the doors. When he saw that, Alberto let loose a paragraph of Spanish curse words Ruby had never heard before.

"Out, out now!" Jackie shouted, and pushed them forward.

The sunlight hit Ruby's eyes and she couldn't see for a second since she'd gotten so used to the dimness of the basement. She could hear just fine, so when her mama screamed her name she turned toward it instinctively. Soon there were a dozen hands on her and arms wrapping her up tight and crying and questions and it felt like the whole neighborhood had descended on them. She heard familiar voices—Aunt Peggy, Miz Trish, Alberto's dad Sam, Mr. Lewis—all filtered through her mama's and gramma's bodies and sobs. Though she knew that she was safe and had been the whole time, Ruby couldn't help crying herself hearing the fear in everyone's voices. All she'd wanted to do was help Rose and keep her safe, not hurt or scare people. She hadn't thought through the consequences.

Everyone's relief at seeing them all safe didn't last long. There was a loud *boom* from inside the school and just as fast as they'd surrounded the kids, people scrambled to the other side of the street, dragging them along. The ground rumbled under Ruby's feet and she looked back to see a small part of the building collapsing in on itself. *So that was Rose's plan*, she thought. The area near the door fell down, too. The entrance turned into a pile of bricks.

Yeah, no one's going in there now . . .

CHAPTER TWENTY-TWO

For a minute it was chaos again. People shouted, asking if folks were okay. Others cursed and still more people were yelling for folks to stay back from the school.

//You are not hurt, are you, Ruby?

She was surprised to find Rose's voice was still in her head even though Ruby wasn't in the basement with her, anymore.

"I'm okay," she whispered. "The explosion just scared people."

Then Ruby heard a voice that made her heart thump hard: Aunt Peggy calling for help. When she whipped around to find out what had happened, she saw her gramma down on the ground. Ruby and Hollie both ran over to make sure she was okay. Ruby regretted everything that had happened that day when she saw the pain on Gramma's face.

"I'm fine," she kept insisting while Mama and Aunt Peggy helped her up. "My knee gave out when I ran, that's all."

"We need to get you back to the house." Ruby could see Mama slipping into her doctor attitude. "We need to get everyone off this block."

They'd ended up in Miz Connor's yard, and Miz Connor fought through the crowd to Gramma's side. "Put her in my van, I'll drive her there."

"Take Peggy and Hollie and the other kids, too," Mama said, then turned to her sister. "If anyone else got injured I'll send them to you until we can get the EMS here."

Ruby thought she would have to go as well until Mama took her hand and wouldn't let go. She didn't even try to pull away.

Mama started coordinating, finding people who lived on their street or a few streets away who would agree to take people in. She matched folks with cars to elders and others who needed a ride so they could leave the area as fast as possible. Then she recruited

Brandon's older brothers to go door to door and see if anyone in the houses needed help getting out. Finally, Mr. Lewis stepped in front of her.

"Anna, I got this. Take Ruby home."

"Yes. Yes, you're right. Thanks, Vernard. Come on, baby." They walked fast away from the school. "Are you all right? Do you need me to carry you?"

Ruby had been too big to carry for many years. This was how scared her mama was and had been.

"I'm okay," she said, and squeezed Mama's hand.

"I should have sent you home in the car. I don't know why I didn't. I'm sorry."

"It's okay, Mama. I'm okay."

She stopped dead and pulled Ruby into a tight hug, crying. "I was so scared."

That set Ruby off crying again, too. She couldn't help it, even though there was nothing wrong with her and she hadn't been hurt. Seeing her mama so upset was the worst thing ever.

"Oh God, your daddy . . ." Mama got out her phone and called him while they continued walking. "She's safe. None of them were hurt, it looks like. We're all going back to the house. Here."

Ruby took the phone from her. "Daddy! I'm all right."

The way his voice sounded as he told her he was coming home made Ruby's throat tight. In that moment she decided that she was never going to lie to her parents again and always tell them what was going on with her, even if she didn't think they would believe it. Even if it was alien bugs hiding in Witchypoo's house. Anything to avoid making them this upset ever again.

When they got back to the house there were a bunch of people in it. Aunt Peggy had brought Gramma to the TV room and already had ice on her knee. When they came in, she was checking over Hollie and the others, asking them if they were hurt anywhere.

When she saw them, Aunt Peggy stopped long enough to give Ruby a long, tight hug and a million kisses. "Are you okay? Hollie said you escaped first, did you cut yourself on anything?" All the while inspecting Ruby's skin.

"No, I—I didn't have to cut anything to get free," she said, remembering her promise.

"We should get them checked out, just in case," Mama said.

Aunt Peggy nodded. "I called for an ambulance."

Miz Trish was alternating between asking Mayson over and over if she was all right and interrogating her on what had happened.

"But why were you in that school? You know you're not supposed to go in there!"

"We were trying to get pictures of the giant bug," Mayson said all casual.

"Wait—there really was a giant bug?" Alberto's dad said.

"You didn't see that huge thing bust out of the school?" Brandon asked.

"No!" He pulled Alberto closer like it was gonna come back.

It was more chaos as the kids tried to tell their story about going in and the adults told their stories about running from the bug all while people were coming in the house and asking questions, some of them about where to send folks they were evacuating from the blocks around the school and some just nosy. Pretty soon Hollie's dad, Ruby's uncle Walter, took to standing at the door and directing people before they could even get in.

"I tried to get y'all help." Brandon's voice broke through. "I told my parents and my brothers, but no one would believe me! I went to go find Mr. Harshaw and begged him to call somebody. The cops took forever to come and forever to finally go in to look for y'all."

Jackie muttered something about how if he wasn't always such a liar that wouldn't have happened.

The only people to get through Uncle Walter's blockade were Frankie Lee and Courtney, who both piled on Hollie so hard Gramma half-heartedly yelled at them to be gentle.

Frankie Lee got her to stop fussing by showing her the live local news feed of the neighborhood on his father's smartphone. A reporter was standing in front of the school—right in front.

"That fool's gonna get hurt when the rest of the building comes down on him," Gramma said.

The feed switched to another camera that showed a caravan of cars coming into the neighborhood escorted by the police. They must have come from the golf course. Soon Ruby heard her daddy's voice calling her name and she ran out to the living room and into his arms. There were only three other times in her life she'd seen Daddy full-out cry, the last time when her grandpa died. Now he wasn't just crying, but sobbing.

"Thank God you're safe," he said over and over and squeezed her so tight.

"I'm okay, Daddy. I'm not hurt." No matter what she said he kept on crying, so she kept on hugging him back.

Other people came in, and she could hear more crying and thanking God from Jackie's moms and Alberto's papi. All she'd meant to do was give Rose some time to escape. Not cause all this pain and fear.

"Is she all right?" Mr. Harshaw came in holding a cloth to the side of his face.

Daddy released his hold on her a little to nod up at him.

"Are *you* okay?" Ruby asked.

"Yeah." He smiled and took the cloth away. Something had left a deep scratch on his cheek. "That thing that we thought took you exploded right in front of us. I caught some shrapnel."

Ruby winced. "Sorry."

"Hey now, none of that was your fault." *If only he knew.* "We thought y'all were out there with it."

"It had us in the school basement."

"How did you get in the school?" Daddy asked. She only escaped answering because Brandon came in the room.

"Whoa, you a'ight, man?" he said to Mr. Harshaw.

"Yeah, *man*, I am," Mr. Harshaw said, and laughed. "Listen, I'm sorry I didn't believe you before. You were scared and I should have seen that instead of making assumptions."

"Oh, uh, thanks." Brandon wasn't used to being apologized to.

"If it weren't for you, your friends might be—" He stopped and looked down at Ruby and her daddy. "Things could have been worse. You saved them."

That put the biggest grin on Brandon's face. He was gonna be insufferable from now on. And he hadn't even really saved them!

"Did y'all catch that thing?" Gramma yelled from the TV room.

"No, ma'am," Mr. Harshaw said.

"It smashed itself to death," Miz Pam said to nods from the adults who'd been there and horrified looks from everyone else.

"The feds showed up and took over the whole scene," Mr. Harshaw said, and Miz Trish practically growled.

Ruby wondered if it was the same government men who came the last time and how long it would be before they came back to the neighborhood and went in the school. She hoped Rose was hurrying up, or else all this would be for nothing.

Uncle Walter came in from the porch. "Hey, the EMTs are here."

"It's too crowded to have them come in," Aunt Peggy said. "Let's take all the kids out to the truck."

She took Hollie's hand and led the way and the other parents reluctantly followed. Ruby's daddy picked her up and carried her—too big or not, he wasn't letting go just yet.

🕷🕷🕷

While the kids were getting checked by the paramedics, two black cars pulled up in front of the house and, just like the day all this began, white men in dark suits got out of them.

"Uh oh," Ruby said real soft. "Rose, can you still hear me? Those government men are back."

//I am aware. Do not worry, I am about to launch.

The same agent who came to the door before—Agent Gerrold—walked up to Ruby. "Miss Finley. I hear you had quite an experience."

Before she could answer him, Frankie Lee came running out of the house, waving the phone. "Something's happening!"

They all heard another big explosion. Ruby and Hollie went to grab the phone while the parents were trying to get everyone back inside and the G-men were talking into their sleeves. The live news feed showed the reporter running away from the school—except the school wasn't there anymore. Now it was just a giant cloud of dust rising up. Inside the dust Ruby saw pulses of light, just like the night she'd been watching Witchypoo's house, and then a flash of red that appeared for less than a second before it zoomed up and was gone.

//Farewell, Ruby. I hope to see you again in the future.

"Bye, Rose. And good luck," she whispered, smiling. Until she saw that the agent was looking right at her. Not smiling.

CHAPTER TWENTY-THREE

A few days later, Ruby and the crew rode their bikes over to where the old school used to be. Rose's departure had leveled the school, and the rubble was surrounded by CAUTION tape. It was weird to be able to see the houses on the block behind the old school. The whole area looked sad and empty. Empty except for the people working on cleaning up the rubble. They'd been covered head to toe in protective suits with helmets during the first two days of cleanup. Ruby guessed that they were worried about contamination from Rose's workshop, which they must have found once they got to the basement. Now they wore regular coveralls, though they still kept on masks.

Jackie waved over one of the guards assigned to keep people out of the affected area. The crew had seen the guard the day before—a short Latina with a big bun on top of her head.

"Have they found our smartphones yet?" Jackie asked. The kids had realized the day after their "escape" from the basement that both Jackie's cell phone and Hollie's were missing, along with Mayson's cameras. When they came yesterday to ask about them, the guard had the cameras—minus the SD cards—but said no one had seen a phone. The crew had been returning to the site every chance they got to see if their phones had miraculously survived the implosion.

"Nope, sorry kid," the woman said. "They're still working in there and they know to give us anything they find."

"Thanks." Jackie dropped her head to the bike's handlebars once the guard walked away. "I'm never getting another one until I'm twenty."

"Does Aunt Peggy know Frankie Lee's is gone yet?" Ruby asked Hollie.

"Not yet. Won't be long, though."

Mayson was looking down the street toward her house, frowning. Ruby could tell she wanted to go in but all the houses in the blocks around the school had been officially evacuated by the G-men. They said it would take up to a week to ensure that it was safe for people to return. Most of the folks put out were staying in other houses around the neighborhood. Mayson and her parents were at Ruby's house. Normally her mama would be annoyed at having to spend so much time with Miz Trish, but ever since Saturday, Mayson's mama was everyone's favorite person.

When the agents had tried to take the six of them away for questioning after the school imploded, Miz Trish had grabbed hold of Mayson and refused to let go. She yelled at them, saying stuff about how they were not allowed to question minors without their legal guardians and asking why they were out to re-traumatize them all. Then she called out, "WHO HAS FACEBOOK LIVE?" and suddenly there were dozens of phone cameras pointed at them. She went off on the men about how they'd caused the problem in the first place with their experimental bio-weapons and listed off a bunch of other dangerous programs they were involved in, some Ruby recognized from the conspiracy-theory Discord server Mayson had showed her. Any other time people would have stopped her, calling her unhinged or telling her to calm down. Not this time. After what the people on the block had seen? None of it sounded bonkers, anymore.

And though the government man tried to keep his face from reacting, a few of the things Miz Trish listed off made him frown deeper—like he knew she had said something real.

After she'd gone on for a few minutes, Mayson's dad stepped up and put his hands on her shoulders. "My wife is right," he said. "You question these kids right here, right now, in front of all of us, or you don't talk to them at all."

So that's what they had to do. And that's how everyone in the neighborhood learned that they suspected there was a metal-eating monster hiding in the school and went in to get proof. All the parents were angry that they'd gone in there alone until Brandon righteously pointed out that no one had believed him when people were in actual danger, so how were they gonna believe them about something they couldn't prove?

"Yeah, y'all never listen to us!" Frankie Lee interjected. Gramma told him to hush.

Once they finished their statements, Miz Trish said to come find an adult if those men ever tried to talk to them again. "They do not have our consent to harass you, understand?"

Even the government was afraid of Miz Trish now.

"I wish I could go get my clarinet," Mayson said, still looking at her house. "Those G-men wouldn't let my mom in to get it after that bug destroyed the school.

I haven't practiced in two days and my band teacher is gonna yell at me. This sucks."

"It'll suck even more later," Ruby said. "My daddy thinks they're gonna build condos where the school was, and he says that's bad for everyone."

"Stupid giant bug," Brandon muttered.

"Nope, not condos," a voice behind them said. They all turned, then spun all the way around when they saw Agent Gerrold standing there. "Once the cleanup is done, construction starts on a new community center. It will have a playground, a gym, and summer camps for kids interested in technology and science."

Ruby got the feeling he was looking right at her when he said all that, though it was hard to tell since he had sunglasses on.

"*Pfft*, yeah right. They been promising us a community center for years," Jackie said.

The agent shrugged. "Let's say certain people are more motivated to make that happen now than they were before." He took off his sunglasses and looked at each of them. "Any of you want to tell me anything else about what happened here Saturday? Anything you were too afraid to tell me with your parents around?"

"My mom says you're not allowed to talk to us," Mayson said, her voice deep with hostility.

"We already told you we were unconscious for most of it, you absolute hairball." Alberto matched her energy.

"And we ain't stupid enough to believe that crap about it all being terrorists," Brandon added. That had been the official story on the news—terrorists hiding under the nose of unsuspecting citizens and building remote-controlled drones. They'd played the video of the school collapsing over and over while talking about it, and around the third time she saw it Ruby realized the footage had been edited. The flashes of light when Rose started up her spaceship were gone.

"You're right," Agent Gerrold said. "It wasn't terrorists. It was an alien."

They all stared at him, blinking. He smiled the way adults smiled when they were messing with you. *He can't be teasing*, Ruby thought, since Rose *was* actually an alien.

"Not you trying to tell us there was an alien invasion," Brandon said, trying to be brave.

"Boy, shut up." Hollie looked freaked out.

"Not all aliens are invaders," Agent Gerrold replied, his voice serious. "Some are scientists who only want to learn more about us and our planet."

Ruby's mouth fell all the way open. He wasn't messing with them. He knew.

"We all saw that thing, it didn't look like a scientist," Hollie said.

"Scientists don't always look the way we expect." Agent Gerrold looked right at Ruby when he said that and held her gaze for a few seconds. Then he reached into his pocket and pulled out the missing smartphones. "We found these in the basement."

Hollie and Jackie jumped forward to grab them, the latter hugging hers like it was a baby. Ruby wondered if the government had wiped the memory.

"Thanks," Hollie said reluctantly. "I'd better get home and hide it again before my mama finds out."

"Yeah, we all should go," Mayson said, tugging at Ruby's sleeve and side-eyeing Agent Gerrold.

They got on their bikes and were about to ride away when the agent called out Ruby's name. She kept her feet ready to pedal. "Yeah?"

He handed her a business card that said AGENT D. GERROLD above a phone number on the front and social media hashtags on the back.

"Get in touch when you graduate high school," he said. "Or before then if you get involved in any more . . . *interesting* . . . science projects."

Science projects, huh? Ruby took the card and nodded. "I'll consider it."

Pedaling away with the others, Ruby thought about whether she could trust the man. His people had shot Rose down, after all. And tried to capture her. He had also said that not all aliens were invaders. Maybe next time they would do better. Ruby knew she would. Assuming there would be a next time, anyway.

CHAPTER TWENTY-FOUR

By the following Friday, life in the neighborhood was returning to normal. The families who lived around the school were allowed back into their homes and there was a big block party planned for the next day to celebrate. Ruby's daddy was in a good mood because he had gotten confirmation that there really was a community center going up where the old school had been. He would get major input on the project because the company behind it hired him as a consultant. He kept talking about how big the budget was as if he couldn't believe it.

The only people who weren't celebrating were the owners of the country club. The golf course had been so messed up by the robobug and all the cars and stuff that it would cost a bunch of money to fix, and the city wasn't giving it to them. Over dinner the night before, Daddy said that the country club might go away completely.

"That would be a *real shame,*" Gramma said, all sarcastic. "Golf courses are an environmental disaster. Better they should put more housing there or make it a park with actual trees to replace the one we used to have next to the church."

Ruby thought that would be good, too. At least a few positive things might come out of all this.

She was standing on her porch watching men going in and out of Witchypoo's house. They were hauling stuff out of there, some to a moving truck, some right to a dumpster out front. Mrs. Reed had come out of her coma earlier in the week and the rumor was that her cancer was in remission. She wasn't well enough to live alone, so she had to go to an assisted-living facility. No one knew—or no one would tell Ruby—what was going to happen to her house. All anyone would say was that it was being cleaned out.

"We can try and visit Mrs. Reed when she's settled in," Daddy told her. "Only if she consents. She might be upset at having to leave her home and won't want visitors."

That made Ruby sad. She wanted to see her again and

apologize for thinking she was a witch. She also wished she could tell her that Rose had tried to help with the cancer. Ruby wondered if she even remembered the bug.

It was getting late, so she rode down to Jackie's house to check on the beehive. They hadn't had to go to school much that week "due to their trauma," as Miz Trish put it. On the one day Ruby did go, Mrs. Bailey gave her back the science fair proposal with *Approved* written across the top, muttering something about how it was very thorough.

As glad as she was to finally have the issue put to rest, Ruby now had a different problem. In the next phase of her experiment she'd planned to capture some of the forager bees so she could test whether they would go to the chemical in a controlled environment. However, she remembered what Rose had said about consent—maybe it wasn't fair to the bees to do that to them, even if she wasn't going to harm them. They didn't know that. What if it made them anxious?

She stood by the feeder in her protective clothing for a long time just watching the bees fly in and out. "I wish I could tell you it will be okay if I take you away for a little while. I really want a high score . . ."

Several of the bees flew off the feeder and over to her.

//What is a high score? Where would you take us? Is there food there?

Ruby jumped back like she'd been stung.

"You . . . you're talking to me!"

//Yes, and you're talking to us. For once we can understand the noises you mammals make. You're strange but nice because you give us food. Is there more food?

Ruby could hear their multiple voices the same way she had heard Rose, half like it was coming from inside her head and half like it was a sound. Whatever nanotech Rose had implanted in her made it possible for her to talk to other insects!

"This is amaaaaaazing!" she yelled.

//Oh no, you are upset, don't make that noise, mammal. We won't hurt you.

Ruby stopped dancing around. "Sorry, sorry. I was excited, that's all. This is new for me. And I know you won't sting unless I attack your home. I'd never do that."

//That is kind.

A new plan formed in her brain. "Question: You know that weird smell I put here?"

//Yes, we know it. Not pleasant. Not like the flowers. We still get food, though.

"If I hid that smell around the area, would you be able to find it?"

//Oh yes, of course, the bees said, flying in figure eights. //We're good at finding and smelling.

Ruby clapped her hands, overjoyed. She would be able to do her project and get consent and get a high score and everything was going to be fine. And even better than that . . .

"I can talk to bugs. I. Can talk. To BUGS!"

//What are bugs? the bees asked. //Are they food? Do you have more food?

She couldn't wait to ask them everything.

AUTHOR'S NOTE

Once I decided to write a book about a girl who wants to be an entomologist, I had to do some research on various types of bugs. My attitude toward them used to be more like Gramma's than Ruby's, but once I started researching, I had much more respect for bugs and a *little* less fear of getting stung by bees. Here are some of the things I learned.

My Favorite Facts About Bees

There are thousands of species of bees all across the world. In America, we're most familiar with bees that make honey, live in hives or colonies, and have stingers. Not every species does!

The ancient Mayan people of Central America venerated the stingless *Melipona beecheii* species, which they called the regal lady bee.

The tropical carpenter bees, *Xylocopa latipes*, burrow holes into wood (such as fallen trees) and hang out with their babies, but otherwise they don't live in groups. They're also the coolest looking bee: all black with a metallic sheen on their wings that shimmers like a rainbow when they fly. Carpenter bees don't produce honey.

Bees that don't produce honey still act as excellent pollinators because they also fly between flowers and other plants to collect pollen and nectar, just like their honey-making cousins.

As Ruby mentioned when talking about her science fair project, bees have an excellent sense of smell. Up to one hundred times better than humans! And they can be trained to identify specific scents, just like dogs. Researchers at the Los Alamos National Laboratory in New Mexico trained a hive of bees to detect bombs with hopes of using them in airports, but so far it's proving impractical.

Bees are so good at detecting biomarkers of diseases such as cancer, tuberculosis, and diabetes that artist Susana Soares (susanasoares.com) created a bee disease-detecting tool that could be used by doctors to help with diagnosis. I don't know of anyone currently using bees to detect early stage Alzheimer's. However, the University of Manchester is doing research with super-smeller Joy Milne, who was able to smell her husband's Parkinson's disease long before he showed symptoms. Wouldn't it be great if we gave bees that job?

Interesting and Gross Things I Learned About Assassin Bugs

The type of assassin bug Agent Gerrold mentions, the *Zelus longipes,* is usually referred to as a milkweed assassin bug or long-legged assassin bug. It's just one of more than 150 different species of assassin bugs, which are a large group of insects in the family Reduviidae. All of them have a curved, pointed mouthpart referred to as a beak that they use to stab and kill prey.

You can find assassin bugs all over the world, including in the southern United States, Europe, Africa, and parts of Asia. They're commonly found in Central and South America.

Assassin bugs can kill and eat prey double their own size! When it finds a tasty bug to eat, an assassin bug will use its prehensile beak to stab, then shoot out venom and corrosive digestive acids inside. This melts the innards of the victim—yuck!—so the assassin bug can slurp it up.

Some types of assassin bugs camouflage themselves

inside flowers, lie in wait for their prey, and then ambush them. Lucky for us, they don't usually bite humans unless they feel threatened and they definitely don't burn holes through metal or glass.

Yes, Spiders Can Fly

In a process called ballooning, some spiders can detect Earth's natural electrical field and use their silk to pull themselves away from the negatively charged surface of the planet into the positively charged air. Up to two and a half miles into the atmosphere! The process is called flight by electrostatic repulsion.

In addition to being excellent fliers, some spiders are great dancers. Look up videos of the peacock spider mating dance if you don't believe me.

Things I Wish I Didn't Know About Parasitic Wasps

Kind of like assassin bugs, wasps can get up to some gross stuff. Parasitic wasps deposit their eggs inside host bugs and, when the eggs hatch, the offspring feed on the host. Sometimes the host bug is already dead by the time this happens, sometimes it's not.

The ichneumon wasp, native to Japan, turns spiders

into zombies. The larvae of this wasp will latch onto spiders, forcing them to spin special webs. When the web is finished, the zombified spiders just wait around until they're eventually consumed. And this is just one type of wasp "zombifying."

It's not all gross or scary, though. These kinds of wasps tend to be tiny and don't mess with humans. They eat aphids, caterpillars, beetles, and flies and can provide a natural way for farmers and gardeners to keep their crops and gardens safe from agricultural pests. In Canada, wasp species have been released to control the emerald ash borer beetle.

My Favorite Insect Exoskeletons

Exoskeletons—aka outside skeletons—protect the bodies of many types of animals. Insects are the largest group of animals with exoskeletons. Insect exoskeletons are composed of a substance called chitin, which makes them very strong. One bug, the diabolical ironclad beetle, has an exoskeleton so tough it can survive even if run over by a car.

Because exoskeletons don't grow as an insect gets bigger, they have to be molted (or shed) just like snake's skin. When this happens, a new exoskeleton grows beneath the old one. It starts out soft but gets harder once the molting is done.

My favorite insect exoskeletons are rhinoceros beetles, flower mantises, and Picasso bugs. All of them are beautiful.

If reading Ruby's adventure has made you want to learn more about bugs and entomology, there is a real Amateur Entomologists' Society (amentsoc.org), and they do have a bug club for kids!

ACKNOWLEDGMENTS

This book would not exist without all my wonderful friends and family, and the support they've given me over the years.

A big heap of appreciation goes to my friend Alethea Kontis, who told me the little writing exercise I did one day was the start of a middle grade novel. I didn't believe her at first, but she was (obviously) super right. Big thanks to Stephen Segal, Valya Lupescu, and Nisi Shawl for offering me incentives and encouragement to start and keep writing. Thank you to all the friends who listened as I talked through the plot and let me bounce ideas off them, especially Christine Hanolsy, the Make Art Not War Collective, and the members of Blackphone. Big thanks to some very important beta readers, Kane, Carson, and Miles and their mom, db mcneill, who offered very useful insights that helped the book shine.

There are so many more people I don't have space to name because I belong to several writing communities that all deserve thanks for helping me grow and learn as a writer. Special shout-out to my fellow Black creatives and all the BIPOC communities who support and uplift so many of us. Community is and always will be one of the most important things in my life.

I can't express how lucky I am to have an agent as wonderful as Larissa Melo Pienkowski, who got what I was trying to do with this book right away. The whole team at Jill Grinberg Literary are rock stars, and I appreciate all you've done for me and for Ruby! Same goes for my amazing editor, Grace Kendall, and the FSG Young Readers team. Grace helped me take this book from good to terrific and made the process of bringing my first book into the world a great one. Thank you.

So much appreciation and love for my monthly supporters and patrons, in particular the folks on Patreon who offered encouragement as I wrote the first draft. Especially Vlad, who left a comment on every single chapter! Having people believe in my writing enough to support me year after year kept me moving forward even on the days when it felt like I was moving through molasses.

This book ended up being a love letter to my own childhood and the care I received from family, both biological and acquired. I wouldn't be the person or the writer I am today without the love and support of my mom and dad, aunts and uncles, cousins, and caring adults in my life. Special shout-out to my aunts Pam and Ella, who have been like mothers to me since my mother passed away, and to my dad, who is very confused by my life choices but always encourages me to pursue my dreams.